There were sounds of hands moving through the scorched and ashed bedclothes.

Nicole moved silently around the bed platform, until she sensed the near presence of another being. She gently placed her left hand around the being's suited right leg and, with her right hand, placed the point of her blade against the leg's covering.

"Put down your weapon, or I will open you to the atmosphere."

There was a frozen moment, then Nicole felt the heat of molten steel lance through her right shoulder. As her mind dimmed from the pain, she shoved the blade with her right hand into the creature's leg.

There was a scream, a blade of energy moving through her shoulder, a whiff of ammonia, then blackness . . .

The Tomorrow Testament

BARRY B. LONGYEAR

BERKLEY BOOKS, NEW YORK

THE TOMORROW TESTAMENT

A Berkley Book / published by arrangement with
the author

PRINTING HISTORY
Berkley edition / December 1983

ISBN: 0-425-06319-4

To Jean

The stars are the apexes of what wonderful triangles! What distant and different beings in the various mansions of the universe are contemplating the same one at the same moment! ... Could a greater miracle take place than for us to look through each other's eyes for an instant?

—Henry David Thoreau, *Walden*

If Aakva is a great fire circling our universe, and if Aakva's Children are still more fires but at great distances, is it not possible that they circle other universes? And those other universes, might they not contain their own living beings? For these answers, I would suffer much. To meet those beings, see them, touch their thoughts, I would exchange my life.

—The Story of Shizumaat, Koda Nuvida, *The Talman*

The preflight literature of every race of which we know posits the existence of otherworld races, and describes the expectations all placed upon their first encounters with other races. The perfection of individual and society all could envision, but none could achieve, each race hoped to find in another.

The encounters happened, each race finding in the other little more than a distorted reflection of itself. Intelligence and

1

stupidity, aggression and suffering, insight and blind allegiance—the universals of life and reality—replaced the hope with cynicism as each race fought for its own advantage by creating rules, tactics, and institutions intended to enclose and defeat the goals of those who were perceived as threats.

Against the stronger powers, the technologically and militarily inferior races formed coalitions, becoming by combination stronger powers themselves. Inside the coalitions, the members intrigued and plotted for control. Outside of the coalitions, the great military and economic powers warred and expanded.

The coalitions rapidly evolved to become the present system of federations known as the United Quadrants. In the area of the Galaxy encompassed by the Ninth Quadrant Federation, only a few of the great powers had not become members of the federation. Of these, the two strongest in numbers, wealth, and military might were the United States of Earth and the Dracon Chamber. Between them, these two powers ruled three hundred worlds.

Late in the Twenty-first Century neither Dracs nor humans speculated in giddy wonder about alien races. They were at war.

1

The learned student has much to contribute to the game. However, the hard truths, the ones that cannot be manipulated, will be told to us by the players.

The players have seen and felt the metal; the students have only theorized about it.

—The Story of Zineru, Koda Sinuvida, *The Talman*

Joanne Nicole sat in the mud of Planet Catvishnu and watched through the haze and drizzle as the distant speck took form, growing to become the bat-winged blackness of a Drac assault lander. It flew low and slow over the denuded landscape like a bloated carrion-eater picking and choosing among countless dead.

She looked at the remains of her command. Soldiers. They sat in holes, leaned against rocks, unmindful of the wet chill of the air and the dark grey of the overcast. She almost smiled as she looked back at the approaching lander.

The Dracs only needed one. The forty-odd scraps of demoralized humanity waiting in the mud for that ship could hardly fill a quarter of the craft's capacity. Forty-odd future prisoners of war; the remainder of a defensive command of twenty thousand.

There was no way of knowing, but millions of civilians must have been slaughtered, as well. The reports that had managed to get through said that Catvishnu's cities on all six continents were but smoking ruins.

A figure splashed to a halt next to her. "Major Nicole; they're coming."

"What?"

"They're coming." The figure pointed toward the lander.

"I see them."

The figure squatted until Joanne Nicole could see its face. Sergeant Zina Lottner; code clerk.

"We finished the search. There's nothing down there the Draggers can use." She held out a silver card. There was dried blood on her fingers.

"I found this in your quarters."

Joanne Nicole took the invitation from the sergeant. The lovely little card sparkled. Amidst the mud, filth, and blood, the car looked obscenely clean, bright, happy. She opened the card and read the raised lettering inside.

The Officers and Ranks
of
Headquarters Company, 181st Force Division, III Corps,
Planet Catvishnu Garrison, USEF
Cordially Invite

MAJ. JOANNE NICOLE
to the
Sixteenth Annual Celebration
of the
Noraanka Dima
to be held at
1930 hours, 21 February 2072 (2651 hours 9/9 Local Time)
in the
Main Auditorium, Storm Mountain

She closed the card. "Lottner, why did you bring me this?"

"I don't know. I thought you might want . . ." Lottner stood, facing the approaching Drac lander. "I saw what was left of your gown. It must have been beautiful."

Joanne Nicole dropped the card into the mud and stepped on it with her boot. Lottner stood silently for a moment, then turned and splashed slowly down the muddy slope.

It had been a beautiful gown; a silly little puff of silver and white—

"How long have soldiers been sitting in mud?"

She turned toward the sound of the rough voice and saw a man sitting cross-legged in the reddish-brown soup. Morio Taiseido, lieutenant, former code officer, present mud soldier, future POW. His companion, infantry sergeant Amos Benbo, kept an enigmatic stare fixed upon the approaching enemy ship.

Hardly moving his lips, the sergeant answered: "How long have there been soldiers?"

The ancient infantry joke seemed oddly profound at that moment. Joanne Nicole looked at her knees, lifted her hand, and scraped some mud from them. She cupped her hand and studied the contents.

Mud. It had the color of blood mixed with excrement.

Mud. It smelled like blood mixed with excrement.

Mud. The universal military cosmetic.

When she raised her head, the Drac ship had grown larger. Does the Drac infantry, the *Tsien Denvedah*, sit in the mud? Do the Dracs bleed, gripe, or do anything that other soldiers do? Two hours into the battle, Intelligence Chief Colonel Nkruma hadn't thought so.

Nkruma.

She closed her eyes, sending her memory deep into the broken mountain behind her; back to so few hours ago.

. . . Nkruma's round, usually impassive face was twisted as though he were in physical pain. And he was. The gleam of sweat upon his dark skin and the shaken voice telegraphed the words no intelligence officer ever wanted to hear.

"Nicole, we must code twenty the command."

Code twenty: destroy all classified documents and pieces of military equipment. Two hours into the battle and the garrison was throwing in the towel—preparing for total defeat.

Two lousy hours into the battle.

She was still wearing her gown. It was indecent. Considering the number of lives, the amount of time, the amount of money and effort invested, it seemed to be against some higher law for all of that to be written off two hours into the fight.

A major battle—the subjugation of an entire planet—should take more time.

More time.

Nkruma had looked down at his hands, two brown-black knots upon the chaos of papers covering his desk.

"I have already told General Katsuzo. He . . . he told me that I was lying!"

Nicole had reached out her hand and placed it upon Nkruma's shoulder. *"I'll take care of the code twenty, Colonel."*

Nkruma clasped his hands, closed his eyes, and spoke in a deathly quiet voice.

"What do the Dracs have up there? What in the hell do they have up there?"

She gently shook his shoulder. *"I've sent the performance reports off to sector intelligence. We might catch it, but sector will come up with new tactics. The next time the Dracs hit a base—"*

Nkruma shrugged her hand away and looked up at her with terror-filled eyes; he spoke with a voice choked with shame—humiliation.

"They're sweeping the entire defense command aside as though . . . as though we are nothing!"

He lowered his head until his forehead rested upon his clasped hands. *"Nothing!"* His head rocked back-and-forth upon his hands.

"Do they read minds? Do the bloody yellow devils read minds?"

Nicole had left the office, issued the orders, then returned to her own section to begin erasing the records. Captain Ted Makai, tactical officer for the Storm Mountain complex, still in his formal whites, sat in the intelligence center, a glass of champagne in his hand. He raised his head as she entered.

"Happy days, Joanne."

"How much have you had to drink?"

"Not nearly enough."

"Aren't you needed someplace? There's a bit of a war going on outside."

"That explains the noise." He inhaled sharply. "No, I'm not needed anymore. All the damage I can do is already done. It's up to the computers, now." She walked around him and began setting up the sequence to dump the memory cores. "Joanne, a century ago this would have been called a complete rout." He finished his campagne in one gulp and let his glass fall to the floor. "But there just isn't anyplace to rout to."

"I'd love to sit and hold your hand, Ted, but I'm busy."

"Busy, busy, busy."

Makai stood, put his hands into his pockets, and began singing "Johnny Zero" as he walked through the door into the corridor:

> *"Sergeant," asked the old man,*
> > *"I've come to see my son."*
>
> *"There," said the sergeant,*
> > *"There he lies across his gun."*
>
> *"Across his gun, you say?*
> > *Then Johnny stood his ground?"*
>
> *"He stood there like a rock*
> > *until they cut him down."*
>
> *The old man left, his John*
> > *part of the battle won.*
>
> *"Yes," said the sergeant,*
> > *"John was too damned dumb to run."*

> *Chicken, chicken, chicken;*
> > *Hoorah for Johnny Zero!*
>
> *He wasn't worth a shit alive;*
> > *but dead he is a hero....*

The deep whine of an enemy assault craft...

Joanne Nicole opened her eyes and looked again at the approaching Drac lander. Erasing the records had been such a waste of time. When the Dracs attacked the Storm Mountain command complex, the memory cores had been destroyed.

Everything had been destroyed.

Almost everyone had been destroyed.

She never did see Ted Makai again.

By unspoken agreement, the survivors decided to meet the Dracs above ground, and had joined the mud soldiers on the surface. Code clerks, cooks, boot-polishers, technicians, programmers, operators, staff officers, and paper wizards moved into the sarcasm of a front line the infantry was trying to establish.

At first there were fewer weapons than there were hands to fire and serve them. In an hour the numbers had balanced. In another hour they had five times as many weapons as they needed. The line never was established.

Now that the Dracs had withdrawn, there was nothing left but the bodies, the mud, and forty-odd sets of eyes staring blankly at the approach of the enemy ship.

Eyes.

Nicole recognized those eyes from the faces of hundreds of thousands of defeated soldiers—in intelligence training, pictures of forgotten soldiers in forgotten places: Andersonville, the Ardennes, Spain, Stalingrad, Bataan, Okinawa, Bastogne, Korea, Vietnam, the Sinai, Afghanistan, Lebanon, Acadia, Capetown, Planet Dacha, Planet Baalphor, Chadduk Station . . .

. . . The uniforms differed, the faces—human, Shikazu, Drac—differed. It was the eyes. The eyes were always the same: the glazed, stunned, defeated stare of a cornered, confused, exhausted animal that had lost its will to resist, its will to live.

The Drac lander hovered at the foot of the mountain for a moment, then slowly reduced its altitude until it came to a steaming halt upon the mud flats below.

. . . *She thought of the tapes she had seen of the interrogations of the seven Dracs captured at the battle of Chadduk Station.*

Their uniforms were filth-covered red; *Tsien Denvedah*, the Drac infantry elite. They did not look so damned elite as they slumped before the interrogation officer.

The hands had only three fingers each; the heads and faces were devoid of hair, the deep yellow skin smooth. The noses were little more than openings in upper lips. Foreheads sloped back, chins receded, yellow eyes stared blankly from beneath prominent brows.

All intelligence officers had learned the rudiments of the Drac language, and the interrogator in the tape had explained to the Drac before him how hopeless its position was. Things could be made easier if the Drac would cooperate.

A three-fingered hand rose and was placed against the Drac soldier's breast. It clutched something hanging beneath its uniform. The human interrogator walked over, slapped the Drac's hand away from its breast, then reached his hand inside the uniform. The human's hand withdrew holding a small golden cube attached to a golden chain that hung around the Drac's neck.

"What is this?"

"It is my line's Talman."

Talman. The bible of the Talmani. The human tightened his hand around the golden cube.

"What would you do if I snapped this chain and threw this luck-charm away, maphrofag? Hey, Dragger?"

The Drac stared for a moment at the human's fist, then it closed its eyes.

"I would have to go to the expense of buying another."

The fist drew quickly away from the Drac, breaking the chain. The human studied the Drac as though he expected the alien to turn into a gibbering column of jelly at the removal of its *Talman.*

The Drac opened its eyes and stared blankly at the floor. The interrogator dangled the broken chain in front of the Drac's face.

"Here it is, you two-sexed shit! If you do not cooperate, I will throw it away."

Slowly the Drac's gaze lifted from the floor until it was looking into the eyes of the interrogator. The Drac's eyes filled with glitter, then its mouth formed into a grin, exposed the solid white mandibles that served as teeth.

"So, humans are as stupid as they appear. I am encouraged."

The interrogator stuffed the cube and chain into his pocket. *"Dracs are the prisoners here; not humans."*

"It is not the first battle, human, but the last that decides such matters. You have just told me that the Dracon Chamber will win the last battle."

The interrogation had gone on for much longer, but Joanne Nicole's head was filled with the conviction in the Drac's words. That and the look in the creature's eyes.

The will to fight, to live, had returned.

As the lower bay doors on the Drac lander opened, she wondered how she would appear to the Drac intelligence service. How she would appear to herself.

She reached into her sleeve pocket and felt for the tiny pronide capsule. Once her fingers had found it, she pulled the capsule from her pocket and studied it. Half pink, half blue, it carried the colors of innocent childhood.

. . .Nkruma had been in the throes of a hysterical calm. He was issuing the death drops in fistfulls to everyone who would take them. As he handed a capsule to her, she shouted to him.

"Nkruma, what do you think you're doing?"

"All of us know things that the Dracs want to know. Duty will tell you what to do."

Duty? The USE Force knew about Catvishnu falling. Before the battle was over, USEF computers would change codes, tactics, equipment, priorities, and anything else that depended upon the knowledge of any person or group of persons.

The USEF *assumed* that everyone would be captured alive, and that everyone would talk their heads off. Experience makes pragmatists out of us all. It also removed the need for mass suicide.

Nicole had held the capsule in front of Nkruma's face.

"What are you, Nkruma? Some kind of Jonestown-Masada freak? Die rather than have the courage to face defeat?"

She watched in horror as he stuck the capsule into his mouth, crushed it with his teeth, and swallowed. After a weak cry, he was dead. Many of those with capsules died with him.

She watched a human in strange blue robes emerge from the lander's bay. He paused at the foot of the ramp and looked up at the remains of the Storm Mountain Irregulars. He studied the faces for a moment, turned to speak to someone within the bay, then turned again and began slogging through the mud toward the ragged assembly.

Joanne Nicole watched him. His concentration appeared to be centered on his footing, his robe held up out of the mud's reach.

She looked down at the capsule.

Pain.

Training had covered pain; the kind of pain made to endure until the sufferer began jabbering—saying anything—to make the pain stop. It had lent a sense of drama to an occupation that was essentially nothing more than filling out reports, sifting bits of information, solving puzzles, and using the known points of a graph to try to predict the unknown points.

Intelligence personnel were "back yard" soldiers; pain was for those filling out the front lines. Intelligence was a job like any civilian job. But there was some disagreement.

• • •

. . .That sergeant in intelligence recruit training:

"It don't make a damn bit of difference what your job is, Nicole. If you're in the Force, your assbottom-line occupation is to sit in the mud behind a rifle and kill the enemy. First you're infantry. You get to do something else only when the infantry doesn't need you."

Puzzles.

She had always been good at puzzles. And statistical analysis and languages were nothing more than puzzles. And the peacetime Force offered puzzles with real challenges to them: alien languages, devising and breaking sophisticated codes, devising strategies to counter alien tactics.

It was supposed to be a clean-collar, predictable, desk job; that's what it had been for nine years. Then, in 2072, the second year into the war with the Dracon Chamber, Joanne Nicole found herself sitting in the mud, behind a rifle, killing Dracs.

The training sergeant had been right.

Damn him to hell.

Sit in the mud, sight through the rain and drizzle down that weapon, and fry anything yellow. No puzzles there; just primitive survival.

The human in the blue robes came to the first of the soldiers, bent down, and talked to him. The soldier pointed listlessly back up the slope. Joanne Nicole studied the man as she held the capsule between her thumb and forefinger and licked the end of the capsule with the tip of her tongue.

The human slogged up the rise and stopped three meters away. The gold glitter of his *Talman* peeked from between the folds in his robe. He spoke in English.

"We are here to pick up those who surrendered." He seemed to be in his late forties—greying hair above a dark brown face lined with years.

Nicole lowered her hand and looked into the human's eyes. "What's it going for these days?"

He looked confused. "What's what going for?"

"Treason."

The man laughed. His laugh was the infectious variety born from genuine mirth. Several of the whipped soldiers around him also laughed, not really knowing why. The human shook his head. "Are you the commanding officer?"

"Yes."

"Your name, please?"

"Nicole. Major Joanne Nicole."

"I am called Leonid Mitzak. Major, please ask your charges to enter the lander. Time is precious."

"What if I don't? What if they don't go?"

"I was led to understand that this unit has surrendered. Isn't this true?"

"If it isn't?"

"Does this game amuse you, Major?" Mitzak looked around at the faces, then back at Nicole. "The fight will continue, if that is what you prefer. If you have surrendered, then have your men move into the lander."

She pushed herself to her feet. "Where are the Drac guards?"

"If you have surrendered, there is no need for guards." He looked again at the soldiers, then back at her. "Is there?"

She dropped the pill into the mud and let her hand fall to her side. "No. There's no need for guards."

She began stumbling downhill toward the lander. One-by-one the soldiers in the mud stood and followed her. There were no wounded. The wounded had all taken the death drops rather than be taken alive to face the unknown. Everyone had heard about the tortures dished out by the terrorist Drac *Mavedah* on the planet Amadeen. For the same reason, many of the still healthy ones took the drops.

The war had killed millions of Dracs and millions of humans; and every human knew what he would do to a Drac given the opportunity. Pain. Endless, excruciating pain. And pronide brought on the ultimate anesthetic.

Nicole paused as she came to the foot of the lander's ramp. There was a red-uniformed Drac standing in the dark of the bay's door. The Drac waved its hand.

"Hasu. Benga va nu! Hasu, dutshaat kizlode!" *Get in. You hurry up! Get in, half-sexed excrement-head!*

And the excrement referred to was *kiz;* an animal native to the planet Draco that was so foul that both the species and the species' waste product carried the same name.

Several obscene retorts in Drac came to Joanne Nicole's mind, but she resisted the temptation to reply in kind. Instead, she moved up the ramp and entered the lander. When everyone had settled on the deck, the bay doors closed, leaving the compartment in deep shadows cast by the lone light above the door to the craft's bridge.

The human, Mitzak, and the Drac went through the door to the bridge, leaving the defeated soldiers alone. There was a quiet hum and Joanne Nicole felt the lander leave the soil of Catvishnu.

2

*The first given is existence; its fact, not its form, nor
its manner of change, nor the purposes ascribed to its
aspects by its creatures.*
—The Story of Shizumaat, Koda Nuvida, *The Talman*

Joanne Nicole awakened from a dreamless sleep to find her
gaze fixed on the compartment's single light; trying to find
some warmth, strength, in its feeble glow. She turned her head
and saw that all the prisoners were buried in sleep or thoughts
of their own.

All silent.

On some vague intellectual level they knew that somewhere
out there the USE Force was creaming the hell out of some
Drac command. Somewhere out there, the war was still far
from decided. But in the total of the universe they could see,
their universe, their guts all said the same thing: whipped.
Defeated.

The compartment light was picked up and reflected by another set of eyes; eyes that were no longer defeated, but, instead, burned with hate. The eyes belonged to Sergeant Benbo.

Nicole settled back and watched him, her eyelids barely
open.

15

* * *

. . . She had just pulled her gown over her head, her lungs aching from the dust and smoke that filled the lower levels of the complex. A dark shadow filled the doorway to her quarters.

"Are you Major Nicole?"

In between coughs, she answered. "Yes."

"Then get your titties covered up, Major. You're in command."

"Me?"

"You're all that's left, lady. Everybody else is dead." Benbo had tossed an object at her, and she caught it as it rebounded from her breast. It was a rifle. "Head for the east face surface, Major. Bring that with you; I'll find another."

The sergeant disappeared into the smoke.

When she drew her right hand away from the weapon, she saw that blood covered the rough surface of the front handgrip. . . .

Nicole looked away from Benbo's frightening silence and closed her eyes as exhaustion again pulled at her. Storm Mountain gnawed at her sleep.

. . . Sergeant Benbo. With curses, kicks, punches, and screams he had intimidated his collection of paper wizards and electron collators into becoming infantry soldiers in what must have been history's briefest course in basic training.

. . . The noise—the sizzle of enemy weapons, the soldier screaming into the hiss of his radio, the others screaming in anger, the few screaming in pain, her own voice shouting orders—sound assaulting her eardrums from both inside and out. . . .

. . . She couldn't see whether the mud-covered creature cowering at the bottom of the trench was male or female. Its eyes were wide with terror.

Benbo slapped its face again and again.

"Get up! Get up on that line, goddamn you, and fire that weapon! Get up on that line, you chicken yellow sonofabitch, or I'll slit you open and hang you by your own bleeding guts!"

A gleaming blade leaped into the sergeant's hand and the soldier's hand flapped in the mud until it found a rifle. Twice the rifle fired as the soldier tried to kill Benbo. The sergeant pulled the creature to its feet and flung it against the side of the trench, facing the advancing enemy.

"That's the way, you dumb sonofabitch! Now try shooting at the yellow fellows!"

Benbo moved off into the rain, and the soldier opened up on the enemy, aiming through tear-filled eyes. Then Nicole recognized him: Lieutenant Morio Taiseido; gentle Morio. . . .

The night of the Noraanka Dima.

. . . She did her best at walking briskly from the corridor into the I-section anteroom; but one does not walk briskly in a full-length ballroom gown.

Too much air resistance. One flows.

. . . the Noraankā Dima; the USE Force holiday in tribute to the five soldiers who had held an entire Shikazu assault group at bay for eight days during the war of the Four Stars. After the five soldiers had been killed, a brief truce was called, allowing honor guards from both the Shikazu Infantry and the USEF to attend the burial—the first Noraanka Dima.

Joanne Nicole pressed the signal panel next to the door and looked up into the sensor in time to hear an embarrassed cough. She glanced down and realized that the overhead sensor had a good shot down the front of her gown. She glared up at the sensor.

"Not you, too, Taiseido?"

There was a mumbled apology as the security door slid open, revealing Storm Mountain's intelligence center. Lieutenant Morio Taiscido and six ranks were on duty. Taiseido stood as she entered, while the ranks busied themselves studying their instruments.

"Morio, why does the Force have to go crazy once each year?" She held out her arms. "Just look at this insane costume."

Taiseido grinned widely. "I have seen it, thank you, Major. And it should make a splendid display at the military ball. General Dell will be pleased."

"Sit down and stick your tongue back in your mouth. Any traffic?"

Taiseido resumed his seat, turned toward a screen, and called up an index of the signals overheard and processed by his watch. "Nothing unusual, Major." He turned back. "Why don't you go to the ball and leave the peasants to sort the signals?"

—A sorter of signals. The next time Joanne Nicole saw Morio he was a killer....

...A break in the fighting.

Toadface backing off from Storm Mountain's unexpected pimple of resistance as the first light of a grey, rainy morning pushed sluggishly at the shadows.

One of the shadows stood up and became Sergeant Benbo. "Have to check the line. See you in a little while, Mo."

Benbo crouched, ran off, and dissolved into the remaining shadows. Nicole looked at the shadow Benbo had been talking to. It was Morio. She spoke to him. "How are you making it, Morio?"

"Okay." *He was as still as the scorched rocks surrounding them.* "Major, all this stuff...battle..."

"What about it?"

"I wasn't ready for it. It turned my guts to water."

"You have a lot of company...had a lot of company."

"Major, I never had any heroes before; just never thought in those terms." *His eyes looked at her out of the darkness.* "Amos—Sergeant Benbo. He is one hell of a man." *The eyes disappeared.* "Sleep. Have to get some sleep...."

...A rough hand shook her shoulder.

"Major?"

She awakened in the bay of the Drac lander. Where every muscle before had been numb, they now ached as though she had been chain-whipped for days. She opened her eyes and saw Benbo squatting next to her.

"Sergeant?"

"In a few minutes we're docking with the lander's..." He issued a single, harsh laugh. "I was about to say 'mother ship.'"

She pushed herself into a sitting position and rubbed her eyes. When she lowered her hand she saw two Dracs carrying one of the human soldiers out of the compartment. "What's going on?"

"Dead. Must've popped one of your bunch's good-bye pills."

"Who?"

"Corliss." Nicole couldn't remember any Corliss. Benbo saw the look on her face. "He was one of the mud soldiers— one of mine."

Nicole watched as the hatch closed behind the two burdened Dracs. "How did you find out that we're about to dock?"

Benbo nodded toward the closed hatch. "I overheard toad-face."

"Adze Dracon?"

"Ni Adze."

"Where did you pick up Drac?"

"Amadeen. I was there when the fun turned from practical jokes into soldier-time." He looked down at the deck. "Everybody talks a little Drac on Amadeen. Then the Mavedah gave me a little refresher course." The soldier lifted his right hand and looked at it. Even in the darkness Nicole could see the pock marks. The Mavedah, the Drac terrorists on Amadeen, liked to use needles. Electrically charged, dipped in pain-causing chemicals; sometimes just for the sake of the screams and scars that could be made.

She looked away from the hand. "How many Dracs are on board?"

"Four that I know of. And that human, Mitzak. Major?"

She turned her head and saw Benbo, hand still raised, looking back into her eyes. "Don't try it. Don't even think about it."

"About what?"

He lowered his hand. "Taking over this lander. Even if we could take it over, the rest of the Drac fleet out there would vaporize us in seconds. Besides, where could we go? Toadface owns Catvishnu."

"Do you want them to work on that hand again?"

"Don't worry about it, Major. This isn't the Mavedah. The clowns in the little red suits are Tsien Denvedah—regular troops. They aren't into pain—just victories." Benbo placed his hand on Nicole's shoulder. "We'll get our chance, Major. We just have to wait for it."

The lander slowed again, rolled slightly, then braked just before the sounds of slamming locks vibrated the hull. The hatch at the front of the compartment opened, revealing one of the red-clad Dracs. It waved an impatient three-fingered hand.

"Dasu! Dasu, nue shaddsaat!"

The human, Mitzak, came from behind the Drac and spoke. "We are at the parent ship. Please prepare to disembark." The beaten soldiers struggled to their feet and began filing through the hatch. As she came to the hatch, Mitzak reached out a hand and stopped her. He looked concerned. "You and your charges will not be sent to the planet Hujiam, as is usual for war prisoners captured in this sector. All of you will be sent to Ditaar."

"Why?"

"The route to Hujiam is presently under attack by your forces—"

"Gee, that's too bad."

"—We could not assure your safety as is required by the war accords."

Nicole studied the man's face. "Mitzak, in your face I see a problem."

He stood motionless for an instant. "Major Nicole, the population of Hujiam is used to receiving prisoners, and the facilities to instruct prisoners are there. The population on Ditaar is not prepared to either receive or instruct prisoners. I am concerned that the Madah of Ditaar will be very harsh."

"Madah?"

He looked toward the other soldiers, then closed his eyes. "Perhaps I can find an assignment to care for you on Ditaar. I shall try."

He turned and left through the hatch. Nicole looked back at the prisoners and saw Sergeant Benbo helping Lieutenant Taiseido to his feet. Sharp fingers jabbed her shoulder, and she turned to see the Drac guard pointing toward the hatch.

"Chova, Irkmaan!"

Joanne Nicole looked into the creature's yellow eyes.

"Ne irkmaan, kizlode. Irkwoomaan!"

3

"When your warriors fall upon the Irrveden, you will capture alive as many of them as you can. Their children will be sent to the Sixth Denve to become future warriors. The ones captured will be told of Aakva's new Law of War, and of the ordeal that proved this law true. Then you will tell them that they may become a part of a new tribe, the Denvedah, and by so doing they may serve the new law....

"Should you capture those who refuse to serve Aakva's Law of War, head them toward the Madah. Say to them that this wasteland is their new place. And that it is a fitting place for those who will fight for neither the Irrveden or the Denvedah."

—The Story of Uhe, Koda Ovida, *The Talman*

"Humans, this choice you have." The fat Drac officer in the brown uniform stood upon a raised platform inside the bay of the ill-maintained building at the edge of the military field, V'Butaan, Planet Ditaar. "This choice to be soldiers for humans, soldiers for the Dracon Chamber, or soldiers for no one: Madah. You die, you fight, you starve. Your choice."

Leonid Mitzak remained silent until the Drac officer nodded

at him and left. Mitzak looked over the small assembly. "Dracs do not hold prisoners. Station Master Harudak offers you the same that is offered to all those defeated by Drac forces. You may continue to fight for the USE Force, in which case you will be killed; at this point, a quite foolish gesture. You may enlist in the forces of the Dracon Chamber, in which case you will be put to work serving the Drac cause. Or you may be neither, in which case you will be cast into the Madah—you will become non-beings, living upon charity."

Mitzak raised a hand and indicated the building. "Because the Dracon Chamber agreed to the war accords, the traditional treatment of the defeated is amended to included these facilities. For those of you who choose the Madah, this facility is available to you for housing, clothing, and food, should you find it impossible to subsist elsewhere."

Sergeant Benbo looked around, then faced Mitzak. "You're telling us we're free to leave?"

"Free to leave this building; not this planet. You are also free to stay, and I would advise staying." He wrapped his robe tightly about his shoulders, and Joanne Nicole thought she detected genuine concern on the man's face as he looked toward the room's open doors. "Out there you will not be under the protection of the accords; instead you will be a subject to Drac custom. And the custom of the Madah is harsh. The people of this city, V'Butaan, are not accustomed to having humans in their Madah. You can expect a degree of hostility from both the citizens and those in the Madah."

Morio Taiseido spoke: "Mitzak, are there Dracs in this Madah?"

"Of course." He paused for a moment, then continued. "There is much you should learn before making your choice. But we are not equipped here to provide you with this education. However, I will do what I can. I have been assigned as Harudak's deputy. I can be found here when you need me." He stepped down from the platform and walked slowly from the room.

Benbo turned toward Nicole. "What now, Major?"

She turned to see the other prisoners looking back at her. Their faces were tired, confused.

"Until we understand the situation, you people stay put. Taiseido?"

Morio stepped forward. "Yes?"

She took his arm and steered him toward Benbo. When the three of them were away from the others, the sergeant began.

"You think it's a trap, Major?"

"I don't know. They already have us by the short and sweet if they want to pack in our meat. I can't see what purpose is served by letting us loose. Morio?"

"Yes, Major?"

"Benbo and I are heading out to do a little recon. I want you to take charge and keep everyone together. Understand?"

"Yes. What about those other two choices?"

"We're going to keep fighting, but if we can walk around freely out there, it's going to make things a lot easier. Just keep everyone together until we know the score."

Sergeant Benbo tapped Taiseido on the shoulder. "And, Mo. If any of these jokers wants to join up with the Dracs, you know what to do."

The Lieutenant looked down as Benbo slipped a knife into his hand. "What am I supposed to do with this?"

"Tell anybody who wants to become a Drac that it's going to require a little surgery first. And when you say it, *mean* it."

Morio slipped the knife inside his jacket and nodded. "You two be careful."

Nicole and Benbo turned and headed toward the open door. When they reached it, they stopped. To the right was a security fence, and high upon the fence's catwalk was an armed Drac guard.

The fence separated the building from the military field. Was the guard posted there to guard the field; or was it there to fry anyone stepping through the door?

To the left was a graveled path leading to a paved road. The bank on the other side of the road was crowded with scrub brush and twisted trees. Nicole glanced at the guard again and poked Benbo in the ribs.

"Let's go."

They stepped out of the door and began walking slowly toward the road. By the time they were abreast of the guard, it was facing them, leaning against the fence. Its yellow fingers toyed with a lever on its weapon.

"Eey, kiz ve Madah."

They stopped and the guard raised its weapon and pointed it at them. *"Zoom! Zoom!"* The guard laughed and lowered its weapon. *"Yaa! Yaa!"* It nodded its head toward the road.

"Benga! Madah hasu, dutshaat! Madah hasu!"

Benbo smiled warmly at the guard. "Kiss my ass, you piss-colored, maphrofag."

Nicole tugged on the sergeant's arm. "Move it or lose it, Benbo."

"Yaa, kizlode! Madah hasu! Yaa—"

"Denvedar!"

The guard whirled around and Benbo and Nicole looked through the fence. Standing there, glaring up at the guard, was a hefty-looking Drac soldier. The thin gold stripes slashed diagonally across its red sleeves marked it as a ninth officer—equivalent to a USEF staff sergeant.

The Drac noncom gave that guard a ragtime that must have been cloned from the first chew-out session the Universe's first private ever received from the Universe's very first sergeant. The talk was so rapid that Nicole could only follow it in parts—several mentions of hot tongs, hand-stoking nuclear reactors, broken limbs, extra duty extending to infinity—the usual.

Sergeant Benbo seemed to be enjoying the performance. And when the Drac noncom had finished, and the guard was again walking its post, Benbo waved at the Drac. "That's telling him, sarge."

The Drac stared for a moment at Benbo, then spat out a single word. *"Vemadah!"* The Drac turned from the fence and marched away.

Benbo watched the soldier until it disappeared into the entrance of a small structure. Then he thrust his hands into his pockets and walked toward the road, his eyes glowering at the gravel crunching beneath his boots.

Vemadah.

The word is the name of those living in the Madah; but it also means "coward."

"Sergeant, what that Drac noncom said doesn't bother you, does it?"

"Hell, no!" Benbo continued walking, his lips pursed as though there was more that he wanted to say. As they reached the road, he shook his head, glanced at Nicole, then turned to the right. "Let's find out where toadface keeps the button that blows up this shitball."

After three hours of fast walking they had circuited the Drac military field. There had been frequent glances from the Dracs standing guard and those riding past them in silent, low-slung vehicles. The only comments came from the children; comments, rocks, and pieces of garbage. But no one stopped them.

After walking the field's perimeter, they climbed a wooded hill to get some altitude. By the time they sat down to rest, they had both come to the same conclusion: the field at V'Butaan was little more than a way station staffed by less than two hundred Dracs.

On the parking ramp there were four assault landers, two of which looked as though they were under repair. There were several small transportation flyers, and no atmospheric fighters.

Sergeant Benbo, seated on the grass with his arms wrapped around his knees, glared in the direction of the field. "Major, if we're going to bust our buns on the barricades, this place would be a waste of time."

"And a waste of buns." Nicole stretched out on the dead leaves and looked through the trees at the blue sky. "The Drac Fleet must have a major base somewhere on the planet."

"This sure as hell isn't it." Benbo pushed himself to his feet and walked toward the higher ground.

As the sound of Benbo's feet moving through the underbrush faded, Nicole continued looking at the sky, watching the spade-shaped leaves of the trees moving in the gentle wind.

It disturbed her that about the last thing she wanted to spend thought on was running around Ditaar slinging bombs around military installations. She felt as though she could have been anywhere, stretched out in the woods, inhaling the freshness of warm spring breezes, the war far, far away. At that moment Catvishnu seemed like nothing more than a bad dream.

Nicole sat up and looked at the Drac landers on the distant parking ramp. There seemed to be something wrong with her sense of duty—or was it sense of revenge?

The civilians who died on Catvishnu were nothing but numbers: the soldiers who died—well, that was part of the contract one made by joining the Force. There had been none of the soldiers that had been really close to her. No one had been close to her since Mallik. And the big issues were nothing but words. Did she really care about protecting the USE's mining operations upon Amadeen? No. Was she in the Force to avenge the Amadeen Front's deaths at the hands of the Drac Mavedah? She shook her head. Not really. Both the Front and the Mavedah were little more than terrorists, each serving their respective bosses by attempting to out-horror the other.

She closed her eyes. "What am I doing here?"

. . . She had been on Earth, in school, aimlessly taking up space . . . but before that had been Baina Ya, and Mallik.

Mallik: fisher, lover and liver of life. They were both nineteen. In the days they owned the world; in the nights they owned the Universe.

He would stand in the prow of his fishing skimmer, his dark brown eyes searching the blinding glare of the water for signs, and she would watch him. And he would call out to the pilot, "High a quarter to port! The greentails run!"

As the skimmer heeled over to the left, he would rush back to help with the scoops. And he would steal a glance at her. . . .

. . . Drowned. They said that the storm came up out of nowhere. Surprised everybody. His corpse was pale and puffy from the water where it hadn't been gnawed on by the crabworms. . . .

. . . Both his family and hers offered to help with the baby once it came. But she left Baina Ya and traveled to Earth before the baby was born. She never saw it; never knew its sex or name. Even the idea of possessing this knowledge horrified her. She wanted no more risks; no more surprises; no more attachments.

She went to school and filled a chair while driving everything out of her head by filling it with numbers. One year, two, then a USEF recruiting team came on campus. And what they promised was a life of absolute predictability; no surprises. So much time in, plus so much experience, education, and training equaled such-and-such a rank and assignment. While that was being done, there are all of those neat puzzles you can have to fill your hours; to fill your mind.

And if everybody gets killed, both the killing, the killer, and the disposal of the remains will be predictable.

It's all in the contract. . . .

Mallik's death had been predictable. Dozens of fishers drown every year on Baina Ya.

But they had been nineteen, and immortal—

"Mallik, damn you—"

"Irkmaan?"

Nicole lowered her hand from her eyes and stood as she

saw a Drac's face peering at her through the bushes. "Benbo?" She looked around for the sergeant, but he was gone.

The Drac pushed the branches aside and stepped through. Its white robe was torn and filthy. It squatted several paces away, its thin arms cradled in its lap. In Drac it asked, "You are human?"

"Yes."

"Of the Madah?" Nicole didn't answer, and the Drac nodded its head. "The Madah. I heard the rumor of humans entering Ditaar's Madah." It studied her for a long moment.

"Do you have any food to share?"

"No. Why are you here?"

"Searching for food."

"I mean, why are you in the Madah?"

The Drac wearily pushed itself to a standing position. "I am only looking for food; not conversation—" A frightened look came into its eyes as the sounds of someone crashing through the brush came from behind. Nicole turned just as Benbo came into view.

"You all right, Major?"

"So far." She turned back to the Drac. "Who are you?"

Its yellow eyes looked down. "I am but another face."

Sergeant Benbo walked up to the Drac. "You wouldn't fight?"

"I would fight," it looked up at Benbo, "if fighting were talma. It is not."

"The path? Talma to what?"

"The path, human. Talma . . ." The Drac waved a hand. "Do you have any food to share?"

Benbo shook his head. "No."

The Drac turned and walked into the bushes. In moments the sounds of its walking died away. Benbo rubbed his chin and frowned as he turned and faced Nicole. "I wonder how many Dracs there are wandering around here." He nodded toward the crest of the hill. "Major, I found something on the other side of the hill."

"What?"

"It'll be easier to show you than to explain it." He glanced back in the direction of the departing Drac. "We'd better watch it." He removed his hand from his chin and pointed uphill. "This way."

• • •

The other side of the hill was barren. That it had once been covered with vegetation was indicated by the remains of a few blackened stumps. At the foot of the hill began the ruins of an obliterated community.

The blackened streets and remains of walls extended for a kilometer. Parallel to their position, the damaged area looked to be six or eight kilometers long, narrow toward the right, fanning out to the left in the shape of an enormous teardrop.

Benbo squatted and pointed. "There's only one thing I know of that makes a shape like that."

"A USEF sonic warhead. Because of the small impact area, it was probably a fighter-mounted missile."

"There's only one impact, Major. The pilot must have been on a for-the-hell-of-it run."

Nicole shielded her eyes and examined the area beyond the blast. "I wonder what the pilot was trying to hit. That's one hell of a miss if he was aiming for the V'Butaan field."

Benbo picked up a small stone and toyed with it. "I don't think the pilot missed." He stood and tossed the stone down the hill. "I think that shooter hit exactly what he was aiming at." The sergeant turned and began walking back up the hill.

Was it possible? Had some USEF pilot gone against orders to wipe out an entire civilian community? Or had the orders excluding civilian targets changed? Perhaps this was only one of several destroyed populations. It had been done recently. And that might explain why the Drac Fleet had leveled Cat-vishnu's cities. Tit for tat. What had that Drac in the dirty robe said? *I would fight if fighting were talma. It is not.*

Nicole noticed the movement of two Dracs picking through the ruins. They were looking for food. Madah. She turned away and followed Benbo's trail.

After an hour of walking, they came down the hill into a part of the Drac village that had not been destroyed. They squatted on a high bank overlooking the streets and structures.

The homes were large, with vast expanses of lawn and woods around them. The distances between homes almost made each home look like a tiny village in itself. One of the streets led to what appeared to be a park or village common.

Half under his breath, Benbo muttered, "This must be the high-rent district." He lifted an arm and pointed. "Look."

She looked in the direction indicated and saw a lone Drac

standing in one of the streets. It wore a ragged white robe and a light blue stripe that went around its neck and looped down its back almost to the ground.

"It isn't the same one we saw on the hill."

"I guess it's another one of our Madah buddies, Major. Why's it standing there?" Benbo's answer came soon enough. One of the silent Drac vehicles turned a corner and moved slowly down the street. The Drac in the blue and white rags lowered its glance and held out its hands toward the moving car. The vehicle hurried past, and the Drac lowered its hands and again stood motionless in the gutter. Nicole heard the sergeant spit on the ground. "I don't think I'm going to fit very good in the Madah."

"Sergeant, let's go down and talk to that Drac. It's about time we got an accurate reading on this Madah business."

Benbo frowned as he studied the terrain. "I'd hate to be a Drac wandering into a human town right after some Dracon Fleet pilot had fried the hell out of the place." He looked at her, one eyebrow raised.

"Let's go." She stood and began walking down the bank, Benbo's footsteps close behind.

As they approached the Drac, it turned and looked at them. At first its expression was confused, then its face settled into an expression of dull-eyed resignation. Before they could speak, it spoke to them. "Do you have food to spare?"

Nicole stopped in front of it. "We don't have food. What is your name?"

The Drac seemed to study upon the question for a moment. Then it looked up at the treetops. "In the Madah . . ." It looked at Nicole. "You may call me Shalda."

She pointed at herself and the sergeant in turn. "Joanne Nicole and Amos Benbo."

Shalda looked puzzled. "You carry your line-names into the Madah?"

"Our family names? Why not?"

"The shame of it. Dah! Something humans wouldn't understand. You speak Dracon adequately; that should help."

Another vehicle came along and stopped next to the three. The driver stuck its yellow head out of the window, giving Benbo and Nicole only a passing glance. "*Chova, vemadai! You may beg here, but do not hold conventions! Move off! Chova!*"

The driver waited until all three turned and walked toward the hill. When they had walked a few paces, they heard the car hiss away. Shalda continued toward the hill.

Nicole looked at the Drac's face.

"If it is so shameful, Shalda, why are you here?"

"I have nowhere else to go. The Madah is now my land."

Benbo walked faster and pulled up on the Drac's other side. "We met a Drac on the hill. It said that war isn't 'talma.' What did it mean?"

Shalda stopped and closed its eyes. "It *is* talma, human."

"The other Drac said it wasn't. What is 'talma'?"

They both looked at the Drac as Shalda appeared to struggle with something inside itself. "Talma." It lifted a hand and touched the thick blue stripe that looped its neck. "Did this other vemadah wear a blue mark such as this?"

Nicole shook her head. "No. Its robe was plain white."

Shalda's hand tightened around the fold of its robe containing the blue stripe. "This, humans, is the mark of Jetah ve Talman. I am a Master of the Talman, master of paths. The one you describe must be very young, as well as very ignorant. To follow talma, one must follow the war against the United States of Earth. I have constructed the diagrams myself." Shalda released its robe and held the same hand out, first toward Benbo, then toward Nicole. "Are you males or females? Except for pictures, I have never seen humans before."

"Benbo is male; I am female."

Shalda studied them, each in turn, then shook its head. "I suppose there is a purpose in it." It held its hand out toward the hill. "I must hurry. There is food to find before the night comes."

Benbo grabbed the Drac's arm. "If you think the war is right, why are you in the Madah?"

Shalda pulled its arm from the sergeant's grasp. "It is none of your concern." Which answered the question. The Drac turned and walked toward the hill.

"Hoorah for Johnny Zero." Benbo turned toward Nicole. "Funny thing; I never thought of the Dracs having cowards."

She studied the sergeant's face. The wall of anger and contempt he hid behind enabled him to function when others crouched in their holes, paralyzed with terror. That and his fear of being called a coward—thinking himself to be a coward.

There was Colonel Nkruma eating pronide capsules in the

name of duty; a duty that was so much easier for him than facing humiliation. Nicole studied herself. She could keep fighting when everything in her head was screaming because on some lower level she was simply following her own rules. *My precious, predictable rules. And I fear losing those regulatory reference points to reality more than I fear the Dracs.*

"There are all kinds of cowards, Sergeant. It's only the honest ones that have to carry the name."

Nicole glanced after the departing Drac, then turned to see Sergeant Benbo looking up at the sky. He pointed a finger. "Major! Major! It's a raid! Hell, but it's the Force!"

Nicole looked up, and after a second or two, she could make out the black spots of a USEF fighter squadron in formation— no, a full fighter-bomber wing! It seemed as though she was rooted in that street for hours—but only a second could have elapsed. Then those specks were on top of them. Benbo leaped, hit Nicole in the stomach, and sent her gasping to the ground.

In the next few moments, the world of Ditaar went up in heat and flame.

The forces of the sound explosions picked her up, shook her, and tossed her back to the ground. Slightly above the thunder of the blasts and howls of flying shrapnel, she heard Benbo screaming a curse. As repeated concussions numbed her mind and body, for an instant she saw Mallik's face.

Then there was nothing.

4

Tocchah walked toward the fires of its people, the footsteps of the enemy warriors close behind. Tocchah looked up to the night sky, praying silently: Aakva, Parent of All, strike this Uhe and its army down! Strike them down in flame and thunder!

Tocchah, receiving no response, looked back down at the path and continued walking, but spoke to the darkness that followed it: "Have you ever noticed, Uhe, that you can never find a god when you need one?"

"Yes, Tocchah. I have noticed."

—The Story of Uhe, Koda Ovida, *The Talman*

...Her head in a vise...lungs filled with oil-soaked cotton, her ears ringing so loudly....

...At some point she realized that she was walking; stumbling down some road through the smoke and silence.

She stopped, wiped the back of her hand across her mouth, and looked at the blood on her hand. It was dark red and thick; almost dried. She wiped her face again. The blood had been coming from her nose, and the flow had already stopped.

"Benbo?"

She lowered her hand and stood, weaving in the street,

33

looking for the sergeant. He was nowhere in sight. She closed her eyes, her head shattering with pain. There was nothing but smoke, and she sank down upon her knees and sat on her ankles. Confused; sleepy. There was something she knew she should be doing, but couldn't force herself to remember what.

She opened her eyes to tiny slits. The smoke drifted to one side, letting her see the fuzzy outline of a structure. She closed her eyes, rubbed them, and looked again.

A large building . . . half of a large building. The land surrounding the ruined portion was swept clean save for a few uprooted smoking trees. The bright lemon-colored patches in the other side of the building eventually resolved into images of bodies.

Mauled, broken, crushed bodies. They were Dracs . . . Drac children. The flames were just beginning to lick at them.

"Sergeant! Benbo, where in the hell are you?"

The pain of her shout doubled her over until her forehead almost rested upon the ground.

There was a weak cry. Almost like a treed kitten. She sat up, lowered her hands, and listened.

More cries. There were several of them. From behind her came the sounds of shouting, cursing, wreckage being moved. The cries came from in front of her. From the crushed building. Nicole pushed herself to her feet and fought against waves of nausea as she stumbled toward the horror of the half-building.

The weak cries seemed to come from there. Closer and she stepped inside the stones of the crumbled wall, realizing that the bodies that she could see weren't the ones doing the crying. She sagged against the stones. Even a Drac needs a mouth, throat, lungs, and life—all of the above—to cry out. The scraps of flesh exposed by the destruction were all missing too many things.

Again the cries. She pushed from the wall and forced her way through the wreckage into the relatively undamaged portion of the building.

More cries. Louder.

"Where are you? Where in the hell—"

Damn. She held her head until the pain subsided. "Wake up, Nicole. Drac. Speak in Drac."

"Adze Dracon. Gis . . . Gis nu cha?" She screamed it as loudly as she could: *"Gis nu cha?! Tean, gis nu cha?!"*

She went to her knees with the pain in her head. A thousand demons smashing their mallets on the insides of her skull. The smoke became thick and hot, and she half-heard the pop of intense heat cracking rock and exploding glass. *"Echey nue cha! Echey viga!"* She cursed, trying to remember what the words meant. She just couldn't remember. . . .

Echey viga: here look. That's a big help. She spoke out loud: *"Echey* means here, and *cha* is to be. I am *ni* and we are *nue."*

God, it rhymed.

"Mary had a little ram, never went back to men. . . . Stick the bleeding verb on the end, except . . . except . . ."

"Echey nue cha! Benga nu!"

There was an exception. Hurry. Always hurry.

She moved toward the dim outline of an oval window, then smashed her face on the floor. Her legs were across something soft. She reached back and felt an arm and a body. She pulled her legs off of it, knelt and faced it.

Gingerly her hands went to her left. "Be alive, kid." She felt legs, then bent over to her right. "Can you hear me? *Dasu.* Get up!" She placed her hands on its narrow shoulders. *"Dasu. Gavey nu?* Come on, kid; get the hell up, Please get up." She moved her right hand up to the child's face to feel for its breath. But there wasn't any breath. There wasn't any face.

Again the voice called: *"Benga! Benga nu!"*

Nicole sat back upon her ankles and turned her head in the direction of the voice. *"Ni benga,"* she whispered.

The light from the oval window dimmed slightly, then a louder, deeper voice came from the window. *"Hada! Hada! Talma hame cha?"*

Is there life inside?

"How quaint. Is there life inside? Well, not a whole bunch, toadface. She shook her head, mumbling "Damn . . . damned if I know."

"Ess? Adze nu!"

Nicole shouted at the window. *"Ae! Talma cha! Teani!"*

She stood up, lurched, climbed up on something shaky, until she was against the wall next to the window. *"Gavey nu?* Hey, sucker! Did you hear me? *Talma cha! Talma cha!"*

"Ae!"

She faced the window, reached deep within the opening,

and felt solidly planted bars. A heavy grillwork was over the opening. She tried shaking it, but it didn't even rattle. "Go around to the other side!"

The wall suddenly glowed with yellow light. Nicole looked behind and saw that the fire had cut off her escape route. Her gaze was drawn down by the sight of countless dismembered children. There was no time to react. The tiny voice called again: "Benga. Echey benga."

It seemed to come from beneath her feet. She looked down and saw a heavy floor grill next to a winding stairwell. Pulling some of the trash from the grill, she knelt down next to it.

"Tean! Hada, tean!"

"Echey..."

She pulled at the floor grill, and when it refused to budge, she ran at a crouch toward the stairs, climbed over the wreckage, stumbled down the steps, and soon was in a huge room, fire dripping from the ceiling.

To her right, large wooden cases filled with rolled documents—huge books, rolled and flat papers—covered the floor. Beneath where the fire had eaten through the ceiling, the paper was blazing away. To her left was a wall lined with more book-filled cases, one of them tipped over in front of a heavy door.

Nicole put her shoulder beneath the obstruction, pushed with her legs, and righted the case. She pulled open the door and two young Dracs slumped against her legs. A third leaned against the far wall of the tiny windowless room and looked at her through half-closed eyes. Its lips formed the word "Irkmaan."

Nicole held out her hand. "Child...Benga, tean. The fire...aakva; aakva..." The words just wouldn't come. "Help. Help me."

She squatted, grabbed one of the youngsters beneath its arms, and lifted it. Keeping an unwavering gaze on her, the third child moved cautiously toward the door. When it reached the door, it stopped.

"Nue su korum, Irkmaan?"

Nicole shook her head. "No—ne. I won't kill you. Ne korum."

The child stooped down, tried to lift the other unconscious youngster, then slumped against the wall, exhausted.

Nicole dragged the child she was holding into the big room.

Half of the paper-covered floor was blazing, and she put the child down in the stairwell to go back for another load. Back at the door, she picked up the second child and helped the third to its feet.

"Let's go. *Benga.*"

They reached the stairwell, Nicole deposited the two children with the first, then she stumbled up the stairwell to see if they could get out that way. As soon as the flame-filled opening for the upper floor came into view, she turned and ran back down the stairs. As she reached bottom, she knelt next to the semi-conscious Drac and shook it by the shoulders. "Wake up. *Loamaak, tean!* Is there an outside entrance to here—*echey?*"

Nicole pointed at the flaming room. "Where? Is there a door? *Gis istah cha? Echey?*"

The child nodded and pointed toward the wall away from the flames. *"Istah."* It pulled at its belt and held out a heavy key and strap. Nicole took the key, grabbed the first youngster, and began moving down the wall. She passed two of those barred windows, then came to a door. Books and papers were piled up in front of it, and the flames were getting closer as she thrust the key into the lock.

"This thing better open outward."

She turned the key to the left, then the right. The lock wouldn't budge. *Hell, the little jerk gave me the wrong key!*

"Queda, Irkmaan!"

She looked through the flames and saw the one who had handed her the key bending over the third child.

"Ess?"

"Queda!" It lifted an arm and made a pushing motion with its hand. *"Istah queda nu!"*

Nicole pushed the key hard, the door swung open onto the remains of a small sunken garden, and both she and the Drac sprawled through the opening. In the distance she could just make out a few dim figures moving nearer. Her lungs were too raw for her to call to them. She pulled the child away from the door and returned for the other two.

The room was a furnace, and as a blast washed her face, she closed her eyes against the heat, her eyes feeling as though their sockets were made out of sandpaper.

Shielding her eyes with her hand, Nicole moved down the

wall until she stumbled over the two children in the stairwell. She pulled one up, threw it over her shoulder, and tried to pull the other up by its arm.

"Dasu! Benga dasu!"

Using her arm for a crutch, the child pulled itself up and began slapping her in the head.

"Aakva!"

"Are you crazy? *Poorzhab?"*

"Su aakva!" It kept slapping her head. *"Su lode aakva!"*

"My head . . ." Her hair was burning! She grabbed both of the children, shut her eyes,

. . . and ran for the door, her feet kicking slowly through heavy oil, the heat taking the breath from her lungs, unseen things striking her head, the chilling wonder of a cold paving stone against which to place her face . . . voices . . . hands . . . an end to pain. . . .

. . . Motion.

In some kind of vehicle. She could hear the hum and feel the roughness beneath the wheels. She tried to open her eyes, but she couldn't.

She tried to lift a hand to touch her face, but her arm was bound. And numb. Her entire body was numb.

"Major Nicole? Can you hear me? Major Nicole?"

"Yes." The word came out harsh and dry. Her throat was on fire. "What's happened? . . . Who are you?"

"You've been badly burned, and the field surgeon thinks you might also have a concussion."

"Mitzak?"

"Yes."

She swallowed, but there was nothing to swallow. "Throat dry."

She felt a tube inserted between her lips, she sucked on it, and a slightly cool, soothing liquid filled her mouth. The tube was withdrawn, and she swallowed. "Mitzak, what about the kids? The three Drac kids?"

"They are alive." He was silent for a long moment. "Three children out of a school of two hundred and sixty." He coughed. "You're being taken to a health science kovah, Major."

They rode silently for a while, the roughness under the wheels smoothing out. "Mitzak, why are my eyes bandaged?"

"Burned. The field surgeon packed and bandaged them. I

don't know your prognosis. The surgeon never said." A sneer crept into Mitzak's voice. "It was very busy. You know, the war and all."

"Where is . . . Sergeant Benbo?"

Mitzak coughed again. "They're dead, major. Your soldiers. All of your soldiers. There were four direct hits on the V'Butaan field . . ."

Nicole grabbed the edges of her litter as the voice faded and the darkness of her universe swam. . . .

5

*Nothingness is a tool of the mind: the useful naught
of the mathematician, builder, and accounts keeper.
Nothingness is not a state either of mind or of being. All
that which exists will always exist; all who exist will
always exist. All that changes is form and the perception
of form.*
—The Story of Ioa and Lurrvanna, Koda Schada, *The
Talman*

Time.

The perception of time ceased.

Darkness surrounded her.

The ointment on her face, neck, and hands removed sensation from them. She could feel her body, but it was as though
her head were floating free of it. It was an almost pleasant
feeling. She was freed from the sensory overkill of everything
that had gone before. Even more, she was freed from the
everyday distractions, allowing the senses she could use to
sharpen, making commonplace things new and exciting.

There would be a buzz—an insect? A piece of electrical
equipment? It was not important. The sound itself became a

41

thing of substance, the peaks and valleys of the undulating waves surfaces upon which she could glide.

    ... The whine of compressors; the staleness of reprocessed air; dim talk:
    "This is cargo I never thought would soil my ship."
    Paper crackling.
    "Read this, kiz for brains, and take good care of her."
    An angry snort, a short silence, more paper crackling.
    "Magasienna! This? This is the ward of the—"
    "As I said, take good care of her...."

    ... She stopped her swim through blackness long enough to remember that sergeant who had explained her USEF insurance and liability retirement schedule.
    So much for an arm, so much for a leg, so much for an eye....
    ... Her first assignment after officer's school, shuffling electrons, keeping an eye on Drac commercial traffic. Intelligence had gotten the word from somewhere. They were preparing even then for the war; putting together the language, codes, slang, procedures, organization, power....

    Dim voices in the distance ... the hum of a strong electrical field....
    ...Analysis of the situation on Amadeen.
    The humans requesting USEF units to protect them against Drac terrorists. Intercepting a message to the Dracon Fleet from the Amadeen Mavedah requesting Fleet protection against the terrorists of the Amadeen Front....

    ... The training officer in alien systems.
    "To anticipate the moves of an opponent, you must be familiar with the rules that govern his thoughts, goals, and actions. What seems logical to you probably won't seem logical to some frog-faced thing that never heard of Aristotle or Boole. But what seems logical to it probably won't seem logical to you....
    "... To be logical is to be consistent with a set of rules. And every race that exists in this galaxy has evolved its own set of rules; its own logic; its own unique perception of the

universe and its relationship to that universe. . . .

". . . The ultimate nature of the universe is relationships, rules; what we call the laws of nature are rules common to most races. Everything else, the whole of intelligent life, is governed by rules of invention.

"Justice on the planet Aluram is a different thing than it is among humans. The criminals on Aluram, as well as the criminal's parents, siblings, and children suffer the same punishment. If the punishment is death, all die. This is not 'justice' through human eyes. But if you could see through the eyes of an Aluramin, it *would* be 'justice.' The Aluramin decided 'good' and 'bad' for their race, then invented social sanctions against the 'bad.' And whether 'bad' behavior is a matter of environment or heredity, it makes good sense to remove those who do 'bad' from the race's gene pool. They have very little of what they call 'crime' on Aluram.

"Very logical. . . ."

Another day? Another week? Another year? The voices would fade in and out . . . the humming . . .

". . . *Mitzak?*"

"*I am here.*"

"*Why? Why are you here?*"

"*It should not concern you.*"

"*Why are you here?*"

A laugh. "*You have become a talma, Major. You are my path out of this war and back to the Talman Kovah.*"

"*I don't understand.*"

"*There is no reason why you should. . . .*"

". . . The Shikazu race of Tenuet founded its 'logic' upon the premise that the Shikazu can never be conquered. The race flourished within this 'logic'—this sense of the nature of the universe. Then the Shikazu were conquered, and now they are extinct. . . ."

. . . *She walked upon Baina Ya again, stood upon the slips beneath the chalk cliffs of Kidege, and looked out to the sea. Her hair blew in the cool salt breeze.*

In the distance was Mallik's skimmer; its silver foils in the deep blue-green water mirroring the sunlight, blinding her.

She spoke into the handset. "Mallik, how was your catch?"

"Good, Jo. A fine haul, but nothing compared to what I will catch tonight."

"Mallik!"

"My scoops will net round, soft, and warm things—"

"Mallik! You are on a radio! Do you want the world to hear?"

"Joanne, the world knows...."

". . . The Timans evolved next to two other intelligent races. Physically and numerically the Timans could not contest the other races, and any kind of physical combat was an early 'bad' to them. But the survival of their race dictated their set of 'goods.' It is 'logical' for a Timan to seek social control over others. And it is 'logical' for a Timan to use such control to manipulate others toward paths of self-destruction.

"While the other races of the planet sharpened their skills at war, the Timans learned how to turn rules back upon themselves. And now, despite their still small numbers, the Timans are one of the most influential races represented in the Ninth Quadrant Federation. The two races that evolved with them are now extinct. Genocide to the Timan is logical...."

. . . The humming stopped. The voices were very close. . . .

. . . Someone handling her arm; a low, muttered "kiz," footsteps, voices:

"Jetah Pur Sonaan, see this."

Silence. A new voice. "The skin should be healing . . . these cracked areas running with red and yellow fluid."

"The human's skin reacts differently to the ointment than ours."

"This was a conclusion that even your master could reach, Vunseleh."

"Jetah, I meant no disrespect—"

"Remove the bandages and wash off the ointment—" A deep shocked silence. "Her eyes. Her eyes, you fool! Hurry...."

It seemed so easy for her to direct her mind away from the threatening, the uncomfortable.

Mind, she would say, look at Mallik. And she would see Mallik.

Move among the stars, mind. And she would see great blinding spheres race by.

She explored the bottoms of oceans, the layers of clouds surrounding gas giants, tangled tropic jungles. . . .

. . . A fog of sound; her head on a dizzy high; the smell of flowers; the singsong that was Dracon:

". . . Joanne Nicole, can you see this light?"

. . . Light? What light? Her lips felt thick and fuzzy as she tried to speak. "I can't see anything unless I open my eyes." She tried to open her eyes. "I don't seem to be able to open them."

". . . They are open, Joanne Nicole. . . ."

Hours or years later, her mind allowed what she had perceived before to be explored. Blind? Was this the horror so many feared? Not to see?

She swam in drug-soaked dreams; seeing. Seeing things she had never seen with eyes.

. . . I should react, feel.

But she was detached from her pain, from her awareness, from her feelings. The darkness was something warm, friendly, comfortable. Long stretches of silence, sleep, and a delicious, drugged something between nonexistence and being. Thought, feeling, and reality were mundane irrelevancies as she let herself drift endlessly upon black billows. . . .

. . . Bursts of light, sound, the taste of copper. The dirt and rock glowing, exploding; the blue streaks of assault landers against the night sky.

Benbo's face floating in front of her. "We lost the foothills, Major. But toadface paid for them."

"How much did we pay to collect, Sergeant? How much did we pay to collect?"

His confused expression disappeared in a flash of white. . . .

It seemed as though she had been treading water endlessly; but she was not tired. Numb, detached; but not tired. And Joanne Nicole took notice of voices. Sound—any sensation—was something approaching a gift. The voices became louder.

"Jetah, the human master is in the corridor. She is a female."

"Send her in, Mitzak. And be restrained. She is Akkujah vemadah and owes us no favors."

Footsteps.

"Your name—ha! Your *skin!* It is yellow!"

"No shit, toadface. So is yours."

"Yes, but . . . I didn't mean . . . your name?"

"Tokyo Rose. And who is this one?"

"Leonid Mitzak, Captain."

"No guts for the Madah, eh Mitzak?" A pause. "Where's the patient?"

Pur Sonaan's voice. "Here, then, is the human you were told of, Tokyo Rose."

More footsteps. Nicole felt a presence over her, then a gentle hand on her face.

"What is her name?"

"Joanne Nicole."

"Very well, you scumbuckets take off while I examine her."

". . . You want us to leave the room?"

Silence, then soft footsteps, as the hand moved and a finger pulled at the skin above first the left, then the right eye.

"Damn . . ." The hand left Nicole's face. "Nicole? Nicole? Can you hear me?"

As she answered, her mouth felt fuzzy. "Is that you, Tokyo Rose?"

Surpressed laughter. "Captain Tegara. I'm a doctor. What in the hell did they do to you?"

Nicole heard Tegara moving some objects around on a hard surface. "Fire. I was in a fire."

Again Tegara bent over Nicole and opened her right eye. "You must be someone pretty special, Nicole. Toadface pulled me out of the Madah on Akkujah to give you a checkup. Can you see anything with your right eye?"

"No."

A click. "Now?"

"No. Tegara, what's happening with the war?"

Her hand moved to Nicole's left eye. "Up until my unit was snagged, everybody seemed to be losing. Can you see anything with your left eye?"

"No."

"Where did they get you?" A click. "Anything now?"

"No. I was garrisoned on Catvishnu."

"Catvishnu?" She moved away; more objects clattering. "We didn't think anyone lived through that."

"I'm about it." Nicole felt Tegara lift her left arm. "Well? What about my eyes?"

A pause. "There's nothing anyone can do about your eyes, Nicole. Maybe if you can get to a USE hospital. I don't have either the skills or the equipment. It looks as though they used some of their own burn ointment on you. The surfaces of both eyes have been burned and stained black. I think the damage might be repairable, but not here. A lot depends on how long the ointment was used."

"What do my eyes . . . look like?"

"Wall-to-wall black." She lowered Nicole's left arm, then walked behind her head and picked up her right arm. "You're going to look like a boiled beet for a while, but I think the scarring on your skin will be minor." She lowered the arm. "Are you in any pain?"

"No. None at all. In fact, I can't feel much of anything. It's like I've been swimming in morphine for a hundred years."

"Catvishnu was a while back. Can you feel that?"

"Feel what?"

"How about that?"

Nicole felt something. "A pressure; scratching on my upper right arm?"

Tegara called out: "Hey, toadface!" There was the return of soft footsteps.

"Yes, Tokyo Rose?"

"Cut the amount of that d'nita anesthetic you are giving her by fifty percent. Understand?" Light scratching, then paper ripping. "Here. Do you understand what that says?"

"Yes. They are common chemicals."

"Make that up exactly as I have specified and spread it gently on the burned areas of her skin—*not* her eyes—every four hours . . . six times a day. Understand?"

"Yes. Can you do anything for her vision?"

"You don't have the equipment; and you need a specialist— a special kind of health master, understand? I can't do anything except to keep telling you kizlodes to stop using that burn ointment on humans."

The Jetah was silent as it absorbed the loathing in Tegara's voice. "What equipment and what skills are necessary?"

Tegara laughed, ignoring the Jetah's question. "Nicole, I have to go now."

"Can't you stay?" Nicole's hand grabbed at empty air, then fell back to the bed.

"No. I'm sorry, but the Madah on Akkujah is full of sadsacks that need me more than you do. Almost four thousand of them, and I'm the only doctor. Once you get to a USE hospital . . . Maybe not. Anyway, the war won't last forever."

Her footsteps and a set of the soft footsteps left the room. One of the Dracs had remained behind. It was silent for a long time, then its footsteps left the room, stopped, and returned. "Joanne Nicole." It was the voice of the older Drac, Jetah Pur Sonaan. "Joanne Nicole."

"Yes?"

"The surgeon who treated you in V'Butaan . . . it had no way of knowing. Everyone has been warned now, but then . . . it had no way of knowing." Pur Sonaan's footsteps faded from the room.

"Mitzak, are you here? Mitzak?"

"Yes."

"I'm not in V'Butaan?"

"No. The nearest city is Pomavu. You are on the home planet. Dracō."

Draco? On the opposite side of the Drac empire from Ditaar? Why? "Why?"

"You have been made the ward of Ovjetah Tora Soam, first Master of the Talman Kovah. The Talman Kovah is here, near Pomavu."

"I . . . I don't understand."

"In the fire at the V'Butaan kovah; one of the children you saved was the Ovjetah's third child, Sin Vidak." The footsteps began leaving.

"Mitzak?"

The footsteps paused. "Yes?"

"The others that were with me in the Madah on Ditaar; where are they?"

"Do you remember me telling you that all of your soldiers were killed?"

"Yes . . . I remember it. Benbo?"

"I don't know. I left Ditaar with you."

"Mitzak, what are you doing here?"

"The Ovjetah insisted that you have some human company; I'm it."

"Are you happy in your work?"

Mitzak moved a few footsteps toward the door. "The Ovjetah is a very powerful person. And, as you know, rank has its privileges."

Mitzak's footsteps left the room.

. . . That humming again. . . .

Nicole continued smiling as dizziness lowered her into a non-caring half-sleep. The smile wasn't an expression of anything; it was just left over from something before. . . .

6

*As do all creatures, we seek the comfort and the
security of the safe path, its direction to be found through
eternal knowns and indestructible verities. But to be
creatures of choice, we must necessarily abandon the
comfort and security of instinct, for all our knowns are
probabilities, and all our truths are doctrines amendable
when truer truths are presented.*
—The Story of Shizumaat, Koda Nuvida, *The Talman*

Blind.

With the reduced anesthetic, awareness returned. Awareness
and pain.

Joanne Nicole began to have a sense of time—the eternal
slowness of it—monotony. The limitations on her universe.

Blind.

It was an affliction from the previous century—harnessed
dogs, bumpy paper, and red-tipped canes attempting to fill in
the chasm left by the removal of sight. She would lie on her
bed, her heart waiting for someone to turn on the lights; to
wake her from the nightmare. But no one turned on the lights.
No one awakened her from the nightmare.

Anger.

It was, first, anger; rage that would have blinded her if blindness had not already become her reality. There were other concerns. She was almost totally helpless, at the complete mercy of the Dracs. What would the Dracs do? How far did the protection of this Tora Soam extend? Who was it anyway?

Deep within her seclusion was a hard knot of rapidly rising fear. If she could only *see* them. The visible is so much easier to fight, to deal with. She didn't even know what her room looked like—what *she* looked like. If she could only *see* them.

. . . At the Kidege ed center on Baina Ya.
She was thirteen, and that gawky, rawboned Mallik Nicole would run after her as she headed toward the Ndugu Wawili transit tube.

"Joanne! Joanne! Wait!"
"What should I wait for, Mallik Nicole? You?"
"Who else? Do you see anyone else chasing you?"
"And why do you chase me? Tell me that."
"You are beautiful, Joanne. That's why."
"Liar."
"I never lie!"
"Do you really think I'm beautiful?"
"Haven't you ever looked in a mirror? Of course you're beautiful! Perhaps not very smart, but beautiful."
"I am not stupid!"
"Asking me if I think you are beautiful is a stupid question."
. . . That night she looked into her mirror and saw a different person—a stranger—someone who was beautiful. . . .
. . . now burned; now blind. Blind. . . .

Days would pass, but she had no way of telling when. Her sleepiness lied; her stomach lied; the pattern of the kovah's routine lied. Empty time became an enemy more dreaded than death.

She would lie on her back, only the sound of her heart beating in her ears, exploring with her fingers the hard bed, the spongy covers, her naked body, and the empty air around her.

She was alone in the room, and if she remained still, she could just make out the sounds of fluid running rapidly through piping. From the area outside the room came only the hush of a robe brushing a wall, a whisper, footsteps.

She discovered that there is nothing in reality to compare with the horrors of the world of imagination. Given the choice between thinking and listening, Joanne Nicole listened.

The soft footsteps separated in her mind and became as recognizable as fingerprints.

Mitzak walked slowly, with regular, measured steps. The heavier tread; that was Pur Sonaan. The light, slow footsteps belonged to Vunseleh Het. It was the one who came regularly to administer medications and read the health monitors.

Food was a nameless, brisk step.

Cleaning dragged its heels and smelled like flowers.

Bedpan had a slow, heavy step and smelled like fish.

The slow measured tread.

"Mitzak?"

"Yes."

He walked to the side of the bed and sat upon some kind of platform. "It's companionship time, Nicole. What do you want to talk about?"

"What were you, Mitzak? Before you took on the blue robe?"

There was a silence, then Mitzak cleared his throat. "Before the war my home was on Akkujah. When the war started, I offered my services to the Dracon Fleet."

"Why?"

"Is protecting one's home too complicated to understand?"

His fingers tapped against something hard. The tapping stopped. "I was a member of the Christian Mission Council—"

"A minister?"

"Priest. . . . Our mission was invited there by the Jetai Kovveda on Akkujah. A sharing of philosophies. We instructed the Jetai, and, in turn, we were entered into Akkujah's Talman Kovah. I had been there three years before Amadeen flared up and the war started. By that time we had been in the kovah long enough to read and understand Talma. After studying the diagrams, most of the mission chose to serve the Dracs."

—*Diagrams. In that flaming library in the kovah in V'Butaan; on the walls, complicated diagrams, logic circles, flow charts—*

"Mitzak, you gave up your religion for this?"

"A simplistic way to look at it. Yes." He was silent for a moment, then he laughed. "Can you give up yours, I wonder."

"I have no religion."
He laughed again.

*. . . A lull in the fighting, and she had heard Taiseido talking
to Sergeant Benbo: "What they say about there being no athe-
ists in foxholes; its true."*

*For an instant Benbo turned away from staring down the
sights of his rifle and glanced at Taiseido, his right eyebrow
raised. He turned back to look for Dracs to kill. "What about
foxes?"*

"You don't believe in a god?"

*"I believe in this rifle, in those yellow bastards down there,
and in Amos Benbo. . . ."*

Besides Mitzak, the only two that talked to her were Pur
and Vunseleh; and their conversations were limited to her health.
And, after a while, Pur stopped coming. Eventually her hands
and face stopped hurting and began to itch.

Between the silence, the dark, and the itch, her mind felt
as though it were beginning to bend.

Mitzak would speak, his voice devoid of sarcasm.

*"Now is when the priest would tell you to pray for strength,
or to think of those who are injured more severely than you.
Perhaps he would call up the image of the crucified Christ,
describe in graphic detail the saviour's suffering, and then
demand to know what in the hell you've got to bitch about."*

"The Dracs have something better?"

"They have talma."

"What is talma?"

*A bitter laugh. "Talma to a human is like relativity to a
cockroach. Even if you could understand it, I doubt that you
could use it."*

She played every mental game that she could remember a
thousand times over. She searched her mind for memories, and
the memories she could find—Mallik's corpse, the burning
Drac children, the thundering defeat at Storm Mountain—chased
her from the past.

She dropped down a bottomless well of self-pity, then shot

back up again with an anger so intense that it made her vomit. In the midst of her wretched mess, she passed out. . . .

. . . *"What is Talma, Mitzak?"*

"It took me months to understand, Nicole."

"Try."

"Nicole, you are in a place. There is a place that you want to be. Your task is to get from the first to the second."

"How?"

"You must know where you are; you must know where you want to go; you must know the limits on the paths between the two. . . ."

After cleaning had dragged its heels out of the room, Vunseleh entered.

"Joanne Nicole, was there something wrong with the food?"

"Why?"

"Your digestive tract threw it."

"Vunseleh, why won't the ones who clean, bring the food, and bring the bedpan talk to me?"

"Talk to you! Why . . . why, they are *forbidden."*

"Do you think I'll sneak bedpan secrets off to the USEF?"

Vunseleh was silent, then Nicole heard its robe rustle as its hands moved.

"I do not understand. They may speak to none of the patients here. The patients would not stand for any talk or other noise. Healing is a time for quiet—meditation."

"Meditation?"

"Joanne Nicole, most of that which we call healing is conducted and performed by the mind."

"Drac, I am just about all meditated out!" She sat up for the first time, her stomach doing flip-flops. *"Me! I* want talk! *I* want noise!" Her left hand hung onto the edge of the bed while her right hand fumbled trying to hold the spongy cover to her breasts. *How much clout do I have as the ward of Tora Soam?* She was in that half-way, I-don't-give-a-damn state between desperation and prudence. "And, Vunseleh, I want to get up."

"Get up? Walk?"

"Yes; I still have legs. I want to get up and walk around. If I lie here much longer, I'll turn into a plant."

"This is a joke . . . of course." Vunseleh made a nervous

clicking sound with its mouth. "I can't have you among the other patients; but I shall tell the Jetah. Pur Sonaan must give its permission."

"Then get it."

Vunseleh's footsteps left the room.

Nicole remained seated until her stomach stopped heaving. Pulling the spongy cover from the bed, she wrapped it around her shoulders, and gingerly moved her legs to the edge of the bed. She grunted with the effort. *How long have I been in bed?*

She moved her legs over the edge of the bed, letting her feet touch the cool softness of the floor. The bed was very low. She leaned forward, pushed on the bed, and stood.

Her head reeled, her legs threatened to collapse, and her stomach radiated warning signals. But she was standing and could feel the coolness of the air upon the sores of her back.

Pur Sonaan's heavy tread raced into the room. "Joanne Nicole, what are you doing?"

"I am standing."

"This you should not do. You are not well."

"If I stay on that bed like a piece of meat in a butcher shop, I will never get well; I will die."

An exasperated silence ensued. Then Pur Sonaan spoke: "Vunseleh gave me your requests. You cannot wander the corridors at will. I must think of the other patients. Also it would not be safe for you. You cannot see. And you are still a human."

"I'll risk bumping into a few things, Pur Sonaan. I don't bruise easily."

"But you are still a human, Joanne Nicole. We have patients and staff in this institution that would attack you for that fact alone. You are guarded here, and everyone in this area knows that you are under Tora Soam's protection. You must stay in this room."

She felt like flopping back upon her bed, but something forced her to remain standing. "I *can* move about this room?"

"... Yes. But *only* in this room."

"And I want some noise. Anything. Can I have a . . ." Nicole couldn't think of the Drac words. "I want some way to hear the news. Radio . . . radio pictures."

"Impossible! Patients do not have such things." Pur Sonaan moved a step closer to her. "Your demands test the boundaries of Tora Soam's influence."

"I want to hear news—something—*anything!*"

"Joanne Nicole . . . I will see what can be done." Thoughtful silence. "A receiver is impossible, but I can have Leonid Mitzak talk to you very quietly about current events. Read to you . . . perhaps some other things."

Pur's footsteps left the room and Nicole collapsed upon her bed. After a few moments of sitting, she fell over onto her left side and slept.

". . . Your name?"

"Joanne Nicole."

"The name of the father?"

"Mallik Nicole."

"And where does he reside?"

"He's dead."

"Were you married?"

"Yes."

"Under what jurisdiction's laws?"

"Planet Baina Ya, United States of Earth."

"I see."

Dull eyes watching line-filled screens as fat fingers scratched with scribers at the glass. "Now let me explain the legal circumstances regarding abortion. It—"

"I'm not here for an abortion. I want the child to be born. I simply never want to see it. It is to be put up for immediate adoption."

"I see. You plan to relinquish all rights to your child?"

"Yes."

"And what would your husband think about this?"

"He's dead."

"But if he were alive—"

"He's dead. . . ."

. . . Mitzak, reading the news out loud, interrupted himself with a fit of laughing.

"What's so funny?"

"The Ninth Quadrant Federation's study committee will vote soon on the question of whether or not to extend membership invitations to the Dracon Chamber and the United States of Earth—as if either would join if asked. It says here that the proposal is not expected to pass the committee. No kidding." Again he laughed.

Nicole sat up on her bed and stretched her arms. "Perhaps, Mitzak, this war could have been avoided if we were members of the Quadrant." She relaxed her arms, letting them fall to her lap.

"A big if, Nicole."

Mitzak continued reading. . . .

. . . The weight had left her. It was as though a tumor had been removed, or a gangrenous limb amputated.

She sat on the grass of the campus and watched the other students. Her face looked no different from their faces. But the way they talked, what they said, the blind confidence of never having experienced any part of life, set them apart.

She risked telling one of them her story.

"Oh, I don't think I could stand not knowing what the child was, or what it would be."

"You would be surprised what you can stand."

"Joanne, sometimes you seem so heartless. . . ."

Heartless.

It was never a lack of heart; it was a lack of guts. . . .

Awake, and again Nicole sat up and moved around until her feet were on the floor.

The darkness. *Damn the dark.* She stood up, swallowed to keep down her chow, then held out her left hand and took a timid step forward. Beneath her feet was the same cool softness; her searching fingers could find nothing. One step from the bed. Another step, and far to her left she felt a metal table.

Nicole went to it—one step, left turn, one step—and began to examine the objects on the table. There were small, capped containers; and she opened each one in turn and sniffed. The ointment used on her after Tokyo Rose's visit and that odor of flowers were the only two that she could identify.

A turn to her right, arms extended, and she moved three steps. Her hands came into contact with the spongy, honey-combed surface of a wall. It was designed to deaden sound, at a time when her ears and mind craved stimulation.

Keeping her hands in contact with the wall, she moved to her right until the wall curved toward her, the room had no corners. Farther to the right, and she felt a row of handles recessed into the wall's surface.

She reached in, pulled on the first handle, and the surface pulled out. It was a drawer. She felt inside and found it empty. The next two drawers were the same. With difficulty she squatted down and opened the fourth drawer.

The smell!

She recoiled at the odor—an odor that whipped all of her carefully hidden nightmares into the open. The fourth drawer contained her uniform.

She touched the familiar cloth and let the feelings rage through her as she smelled the filth from her body, the dried mud of Catvishnu, the smoke from the burning school, and that Drac burn ointment that had blinded her.

That chasm of self-pity yawned before her again, and she sat on the floor and let herself tumble in. She felt the tears run down her cheeks and splash on her lap. She touched the place where the tears had fallen and told herself that she was naked. She was naked and didn't care.

The footsteps of Pur Sonaan and Vunseleh Het entered the room to her right. Pur Sonaan's voice spoke sharply to Vunseleh.

"Empty head! Find her a robe to wear!"

"Yes, Jetah."

Vunseleh's footsteps left the room. Pur Sonaan stood silently for a moment. Then it moved, and Nicole felt a cloth in a hand drying her lap, drying the tears from her face.

"Why did you keep my uniform? Why?"

"It belongs to you. We need your permission to dispose of it."

"Throw it out! Throw it *out!*"

Nicole pushed the drawer shut and let her hands fall to her lap. "Pur Sonaan, you are a Drac. You have to hate humans, don't you?" She let the words hang in the air as she let her mouth form for the first time the words her mind would not allow herself to think. "Give me something."

"Something, Joanne Nicole?"

"Anything that will *kill* me."

She sensed the Jetah stand upright. Pur said nothing for long, strained moments; its breath coming in rapid hisses. Then it answered. "You think this to be a small favor you ask? You ask me to *soil* myself, Joanne Nicole! *Never* do so again!"

She felt its hands beneath her shoulders as it easily lifted her to her feet and led her to the bed. Nicole sat on the bed, her feet on the floor, her eyes dribbling more tears. "Pur Sonaan?"

"Yes?"

"If I am so important to this Tora Soam character, why does it never come to see me?"

Pur Sonaan snorted out a brief laugh. "Tora Soam is Ovjetah of the Talman Kovah. The demands on its time, especially because of the war, are tremendous. But Tora Soam asks about you when it can...as does Sin Vidak, the child you saved. Did you know...that Sin Vidak has now entered training for the Tsien Denvedah?"

Nicole sat back, stunned. "The Tsien Denvedah? That little child?" *Did I pull its narrow yellow ass out of the flames to provide fodder for the Drac meatgrinder? To hit the dirt in a little red suit and kill humans?* "Sin Vidak *has* to be too young!"

"Joanne Nicole, Dracs reach adulthood in approximately a fifth of the time it takes humans."

"I know, but still..."

"Sin Vidak is an adult now." Pur Sonaan paused. "It has been a long time since you were in V'Butaan." A long time.

"How long? In my time?"

Much later, Mitzak was sent in with the information. It had been twenty months since V'Butaan. Twenty months.

How could...how could I have lost almost two years?

She felt folds of cloth placed into her hands. "Here is your robe. Do you want me to help you put it on?"

"No."

Mitzak left the room to be replaced by Pur Sonaan. Nicole used the palm of her right hand to wipe the wetness from her face.

The Drac spoke. "There is something I must say. Joanne Nicole, your life is your own property, and ending it is your right and your choice. But should you choose to end it, you must realize that the exercise of such a right is your own task. Never ask another to perform it for you."

Pur Sonaan's heavy footsteps left the room, and Joanne Nicole placed her face upon the bed.

She damned herself for her tears. But there was a little yellow child who was earning the right to proudly wear the red of the Tsien Denvedah, and there had to be tears.

7

"Curse the mistakes, rail at them, regret them, learn from them. But do not wish for the perfection of time when mistakes will no longer be made, for that is what we call death."
—The Story of Cohneret, Koda Tarmeda, *The Talman*

The next day on the floor, as Nicole tried to exercise, she listened to Mitzak reading the news.

"This is strange."

"What's strange, Mitzak?"

"The Ninth Quadrant study committee voted down the invitations—"

"Just as you said they would."

"—but the vote was very close. Much closer than I expected. And Hissied-do'Timan—delegate from Timan—was the only abstention." Mitzak was silent for a long time.

"What are you thinking about?"

A pause, then the sounds of Mitzak rearranging himself in his chair. "I don't understand the reason for this abstention."

"Who can figure a Timan, Mitzak? Most of them are so wrapped up wheeling and dealing I doubt if they know themselves what they're doing half of the time." After straining herself to do another situp, Nicole flopped flat on her back. "Mitzak, is there any news on the war?"

"Always."

A silence, then he continued reading. "This day Het Kraakar, First Warmaster of the Dracon Fleet, announced through its representative that the Planet Ditaar has fallen to the forces of the United States of Earth. Figures on military and civilian casualties . . ."

Nicole heard him stand. "Excuse me." His footsteps left the room.

Alone, listening to footsteps. It was cleaning. Nicole sat up. "Are you allowed to speak to me now?"

"Yes. Yes I am." The voice was quiet, nervous, meek. "I would have talked much sooner—I have so many questions— but silence here is the rule."

"I understand."

"Joanne Nicole?"

"Yes—what is your name?"

"Vencha Eban. Joanne Nicole? Could you get up on the bed so that I can clean?"

"Of course."

Nicole nodded, reached to the bed, and pulled herself to her feet. She retrieved her robe from the bed and pulled it on over her head, letting the cape wrap around her left arm. Sitting on the bed, she pulled up her feet.

"Vencha Eban, where can I take a shower? Clean myself?"

"There is a place attached to this room." More footsteps, going to her right. "The door is locked. Perhaps you are not to wash until the healing of your skin is complete."

"I would still like to stop using the bedpan. I can get around sufficiently."

Nicole heard a door open. "The waste room is open for you."

"Good."

A series of bruises and barked shins had discouraged her from exploring that portion of the room very far, and all that she had found was the door that was locked.

"Jetah Pur Sonaan said it was very important that I talk to you, Joanne Nicole. Is there something is particular you wish to hear?"

"No. Anything." She thought for a moment about Mitzak's

self-righteous attitude concerning talma. "Do you know anything about *The Talman?*"

"Of course. Reciting it is part of the right of adulthood."

"Reciting it? The entire thing?"

"Yes. Would you like to hear a recitation?"

"Yes."

"Is there any particular part you would like to hear?"

"No, Vencha Eban. Pick whatever you want. I just want noise."

"It is *not* just noise."

"I know. I meant no offense. Go on."

"I will recite 'The Story of Shizumaat' while I am cleaning. It is one of my favorites. You must remember that I speak this story as Namndas, the narrator of Shizumaat's story."

"I understand."

As the tinny hum of cleaning continued in the room, Vencha Eban recited:

"I speak these things of Shizumaat to you; for I am Namndas, the friend of Shizumaat; the one who stood and waited at the mark.

"And this is my teacher's story: The firstborn of Sindieah Nu was Sindieah Ay. After its parent had retired from the servants, and during Sindieah Ay's rule of the servants of Aakva, the Temple of Uhe was completed.

"The cut-stone walls of the temple were as tall as eight Sindie and they enclosed an area of sixty by ninety paces. The roof of wooden beams and slabstone was supported by square stone columns arranged in six proportionate rectangles.

"At the center of the smallest rectangle was the great stone tomb that covered Uhe's ashes. The eastern wall of the temple was an open row of stone columns. Northern and southern walls each had center doorways only two paces wide. The wall facing the Madah had no opening...."

Madah, Nicole thought to herself. *What is the Madah?*

"During the day, light was provided by Aakva, the Parent of All; during the night, light was provided by the nine hundred oil lamps that were suspended from the temple's great ceiling

"The shelters around the temple were separated by narrow streets, and were made of both stone and wood. In one of these houses, covered by the afternoon shadow of the temple, a

Sindie shaper of iron that was in Butaan to perform its duty to Aakva through labor gave birth to a child.

"The shaper of iron's name was Caduah; and Caduah named its child Shizumaat.

"On the beginning of Shizumaat's third year, Caduah entered its child in the temple to perform before the servants the rites of adulthood. Shizumaat recited the story of creation, the laws, and the story of Uhe; and then Shizumaat recited its family line from its parent, Caduah, to the founder of its line, the Mavedah hunter called Limish. . . ."

Madah, again, thought Nicole. *Except this time it is not vemadah; it's Mavedah. The same name used by the Drac terrorists on Amadeen.*

"And when the rites were completed, Caduah applied for Shizumaat to become a servant of Aakva.

"Ebneh was the servant who had heard the child's recitation, and Ebneh was sufficiently impressed by the performance that it enrolled Shizumaat into the Aakva Kovah.

"The nights Shizumaat would spend in its parent's house; the days Shizumaat would spend in the temple learning the secrets, signs, laws, wishes, and visions of the Parent of All.

"I, Namndas, had entered the Aakva Kovah the year before Shizumaat, and was placed in charge of Shizumaat's class. I drew this duty because the servants of the temple considered me the least worthy of my own class. While my companions sat at the feet of the servants and engaged in learned discourse, I would chase dirt—"

Vencha laughed. It was not hard to see who Vencha identified with. Tail-End Charlie; the hind teat; the ten percent that never gets the word.

Nicole smiled. *Namndas was a creature of the Universe, and it had lots of human company.*

Vencha Eban, as Namndas, continued:

"My charges were assigned a place in the darkness next to the Madah wall of the temple, where my own class had begun the year before. On the morning of the first day of their instruction, they sat upon the smooth stone floor and listened as I spoke the rules of the temple.

"'I, Namndas, am your charge-of-class. You are the lowest class in the temple, and for this reason, the care and cleaning of the temple is left to you. I tell you now that I will never find as much as a single fleck of dust in the temple while I am your charge-of-class. You will clean the filth from the air before it lands upon these stones; you will wash the dust from the feet of those who enter the temple.'

"I pointed toward the soot-blackened ceiling. 'Every evening it is your responsibility to trim and fuel the temple's lamps. Through all of this, you will keep clean yourselves.'

"Shizumaat stood. It was tall for its age, and there was a strange brightness to its eyes. 'Namndas, when are we to be given our instruction? When will we learn?'

"I felt my face grow hot. Such impudence! 'You shall be allowed to receive instruction when I inform Servant Ebneh that you are worthy. Sit and be silent!' Shizumaat resumed its seat upon the floor, and I issued a glare that encompassed all nine of the students. 'You will not speak except in answer to a question from me or from one of the servants. You are here to learn, and the first thing you must learn is obedience.'

"I narrowed my glare to Shizumaat and saw it carrying an enigmatic expression upon its face. I spoke to Shizumaat. 'I cannot read your face, new-charge. What does it say?'

"Shizumaat remained seated upon the floor, but looked at me as it spoke. 'Does Aakva, then, judge its servants by how well they imitate the dumb animals and their skill at wielding a scrub rag?'

"'Your words court disaster.'

"'Namndas, when you asked your question, did you want from me lies or truth?'

"'This is a temple of truth. What are you called?'

"'I am called Shizumaat.'

"'Then, Shizumaat, I must tell you that I see little hope for your graduation from the Madah wall to the center of the temple.'

"Shizumaat nodded and looked toward Uhe's tomb. 'I think the truth serves you at last, Namndas—'"

Nicole heard Pur Sonaan's heavy footsteps enter the room, and there followed a delightful, horrified little gasp out of Vencha Eban. No words were exchanged, but Nicole's skin virtually tingled with what she sensed to be highly meaningful glances between the Jetah and Vencha Eban.

"Do you have cleaning to do?"

"Yes, Jetah. I was just resting for a moment."

"Emmm."

The sounds of vigorous cleaning began.

Nicole spoke to the Jetah. "Is there anything new concerning my eyes?"

The Jetah sighed. "The more we learn, the closer we get; and the closer we get, the more there is to learn. The anatomy of the human eye is considerably different than ours, and human eyes for experimentation are not easy to come by."

She sat up. *"What?!"*

"No! No! The kovah takes them only from the dead. I assure you. And we have been getting more information from captured medical texts, and from the USEF itself through the provisions of the war accords." The Jetah paused for a moment. "I must tell you that we have an instrument that we can use on Drac patients who have been blinded. Implants are placed into the vision centers of the patient's brain, and this enables the patient to see using gelatinous receivers that fit over the eyes."

Nicole heard Vencha Eban turn off its equipment and steal quietly out of the room.

"Can you . . . can you do this for me?"

"As a last resort we might try. The procedure is well-established and quite common. However, we only use it when the sensory nerves leading from the eye have been destroyed. We have no reason to believe that yours have been damaged."

"Pur Sonaan, would making those implants injure my optic nerves?"

"Probably. And the brain scans we have made have shown us that the differences—chemical, electrical, and structural— between human and Drac neural systems are considerable. Not only might not the procedure work with you, it might damage your vision centers beyond any repair. It might even kill you. We are planning nothing at present; I am just keeping you informed."

Time for a new subject. "Pur Sonaan, I heard the word 'Madah' and 'Mavedah' used in that story Vencha Eban was reciting."

"Yes?"

"Both Mavedah and vemadah mean 'of the Madah.' But

what is the difference between sticking the 'of' in front or in the middle of the word?"

"It is the difference between modern usage and ancient formal usage. Vencha was reciting the Nuvida. You should begin earlier, with the Koda Sinda, The Myth of Aakva. Go straight to *The Talman* itself."

Nicole smiled. "How do I do that?"

"Emmmm. I have a player. If I bring you my personal player will you use it quietly? I cannot have the other patients disturbed."

"Yes. Yes, I'll be very quiet."

> ... And Aakva was said to make on the world special creatures of yellow skin and hands and feet each of three fingers. And it was said to make the creatures of one kind, that each could bear its young, or the young of another. And it was said to make the creatures stand upright, make thought, and give voice that the creatures could worship the Parent of All.

> *Sindie was the world.*
> *And the World was said to be made by Aakva, the God of the Day Light....*

It took very little time for Nicole to realize that *The Talman* began with the oldest written document known to the Drac race. The Myth of Aakva and The Story of Uhe both predated the Drac ancestral planet's year dating system. Sindie was the ancestral planet, and year dates on that planet began with the birth of Shizumaat eleven thousand eight hundred and seventy-two of Sindie's years ago. When Nicole asked, Mitzak informed her that Shizumaat was born in 9679 BC.

The Myth was a Book of Genesis for hermaphrodites. It described the creation of the race and Aakva's reason for the creation. In addition, it placed a priesthood firmly in control of everything.

> ... And the first chief of servants was named Rhada.
> Rhada had the servants go among the Sindie and learn all of the signs and visions that were known. And the servants gathered this knowledge and gave it to Rhada.

For twelve days and twelve nights, the chief of the servants studied the signs and visions, and sorted the false from the true, the tribal lays from the true Laws of Aakva.

And on the thirteenth day, Rhada spoke to the servants what it had learned. . . .

And Rhada ordered the servants to go among the Sindie and teach the Laws. And it was promised by Rhada that for just so long as the Sindie listened to Aakva's servants and followed the laws the God of the Day Light made, there would be peace and plenty.

And the Sindie listened to the servants, learned the laws, and followed the laws. They made sacrifice to Aakva through its servants. . . .

An old political structure: theocratic despotism. Pay your way into Heaven. But there was something about the verb tense used in The Myth of Aakva.

"And the world was *said* to be made by Aakva . . ." "It was *said* that Aakva called its children the Sindie . . ."

It was not stated as fact; it was stated as theological heresay. It was there to show beginnings. Nicole continued listening. There were many stories within the Myth: Summat, the doubter Daultha, Aakva's curse of war upon the Sindie, Aakva's division of the Sindie into the four great tribes.

She thought upon the universality of certain things: explanations, ideals, hopes. She picked up the tiny player, pulled herself out of bed, and began to walk the room as she listened to the Koda Ovida, The Story of Uhe.

It began with an explanation of the tabus that kept the four tribes from war. It continued with a story that began in a land . . . a land called the Madah.

Almost twelve thousand years ago, in a patch of hilly desert, before the world of Sindie was known to be a world, there was the Madah. It was a land of drought and famine.

The tribe of the Madah, the Mavedah, had been reduced to eating its own dead . . .

She heard Vunseleh's footsteps enter the room, and moved to turn off the player. "Please, Joanne Nicole. Leave the story run. The reciter is Higa Tidanoa. Get on the bed, I shall apply your ointment, and we shall both listen."

She removed her robe and sat naked upon the bed. The story continued.

Near a fire was one of the lower servants of Aakva named Uhe. And that night Uhe sat and watched as its only child, Leuno, died of starvation. And Uhe watched as the food preparers carried Leuno's small body toward the masters' fire.

Uhe said to the God of the Day Light:

"This, then, is your promise of plenty for keeping your Law of Peace, Aakva? Is this the mercy and reward of the Parent of All?"

Silence answered Uhe that night. And Uhe saw a child gnawing upon a piece of cured tent skin, while the child's parent, a once proud hunter, watched with envy in its eyes. Near one of the hunters' fires, eight sat waiting for a child to make its last breath. When that breath ended, the pitifully wasted corpse would be apportioned among the hunters.

Uhe studied the faces of the hunters and saw that one of them was mouthing the curse of quick death. And the curse was for the child. And the one who cursed was the parent. And there was nothing but hunger in the parent's eyes.

Rage drove the pain and fear from Uhe's head. It was before that first night's fire, the land still warm from Aakva's touch, that Uhe stood before the tribe's masters.

Uhe said:

"Bantumeh, great and honored ruler of the masters of the Mavedah, this night you have tasted the flesh of my child, Leuno."

And Bantumeh covered its face with its hands. "Your shame is our shame, poor Uhe."

Bantumeh uncovered a face wrinkled with age, pain, and the scars of many challenges to the rulership of the Mavedah.

"But we have all tasted either child, sibling, parent, or friend this year. There is no choice. To put our minds aside as we eat to keep the Mavedah alive is our sole hope. Your grief is understood; your reminder is out of place."

At the rebuke Uhe did not retire from the ring of

masters, but instead pointed east toward the Akkujah Mountains. "There, Bantumeh, is food for the Mavedah."

Bantumeh stood, its face crossed with anger. "You would have the Mavedah violate the tabus? Could we do such a thing, do you not think that I would already have done it?"

A master named Iyjiia, who was the chief of Aakva's servants, leaped to its feet.

"Uhe, this is a beast standing before the masters, not a servant of Aakva!" Iyjiia faced the other masters and filled its image with voice, for Iyjiia was thin and small in stature.

"The law is clear. The Mavedah is forbidden to enter the domain of the Irrvedan, just as the Irrveden is forbidden to enter the Madah. It is tabu even for us to ask the Irrveden for food."

Iyjiia faced Uhe and pointed. "Even to *wish* this is tabu!"

Most of the masters nodded and muttered their agreement. It was a painful law to obey, but its wisdom was understood by all. To violate that law would again bring the wars to Sindie. This was the promise of Aakva, and the wars were too horrible to contemplate.

Uhe held out its arms and faced the night sky. "But I invoke a new vision from Aakva. Its old law was for a time and a place. Aakva speaks to me that the time is changed. And Aakva speaks to us all that the place is changed. It is time for a new law."

Iyjiia stood silent, for there was danger in disputing one's claim to a vision. If the claim of the young Uhe were false, Uhe would suffer for it. But Iyjiia would pay the same price if it disputed a vision that turned out to be true law.

Iyjiia also saw that many members of the tribe had gathered around the ring of masters. Whether the law be true or not, if it promised food it might find support among that gathering crowd of armed hunters.

Iyjiia returned to its place in the ring of masters and said to Uhe, "Tell us your vision."

As was the custom, Uhe unfastened its covering of

skins and stood naked before them to show the truth of its words.

"Aakva speaks to me now. It speaks of lush mountains to the east, where the darghat and the suda kneel to drink at the plentiful waters; where the trees are heavy with sweet fruits; the fields crowded with kadda melon and the white grain.

"Every evening Aakva's hands of fire point beyond those mountains. It shows me the Diruvedah and the Kuvedah, their bellies bloated with fresh-cooked flesh; their grasslands crowded with game that leaps upon their spears; their children tall and laughing.

"Then Aakva points west of the mountains to this land of famine and the God of the Day Light says to me, 'Uhe, this is my sign that the Mavedah must leave this place. The masters of the Mavedah must go to their peoples, tell them of Aakva's Law of War, and have them gather at the foot of the Akkujah Mountains where the cliffs of Akkujah fall to the Yellow Sea.

"From there I will lead the Mavedah across the mountains, through the land of the Irrveden, to the Dirudah. And the Mavedah will defeat the Diruvedah and will drive the Irrveden from the Great Cut and the southern Akkujah into the northern mountains."

Uhe stopped speaking, but it remained with arms outstretched. Uhe's voice became low and grave as it continued.

"The Irrveden will try to join with the Kuvedah against us. But too fast will we attack. With the blood command of Aakva at our backs, we will strike north through the mountains, brushing the Irrveden aside. And then we will flood the lands of the Kuvedah with our victories! The Mavedah will rule all!"

Uhe lowered its arms, then stooped and retrieved its covering of skins. With its coverings replaced, Uhe faced Iyjiia. "And that is what the God of the Day Light says to me."

Bantumeh studied Uhe. "Wars? Are we to believe that the God of Day Light inflicts this ancient punishment upon us? What have we done?"

Uhe bowed. "Bantumeh, you are kind and wise. But

you are too kind to meet this need of the Mavedah. It matters not what we have done. The old law will see the end of the Mavedah. Aakva's new Law of War will see us, our children, and the Mavedah live."

Uhe talked to the masters and to the hunters crowded about the fire.

"I see there to be things *worse than war*. I see our glorious hunters grubbing in the dirt; I see the Mavedah eating now things too low to rank with waste; I see the Mavedah eating now things too precious and sacred to be food. And I see from this the end of the Mavedah."

Uhe faced the ruler of the Mavedah. "Bantumeh, there *are* things worse than war."

Iyjiia stood and waved its hands back and forth. "You cannot know this, Uhe. The oldest of us has never seen war. And this is only because we all obey the tabus."

Uhe faced Iyjiia.

"Mavedah does not fight Mavedah. Once there is nothing but Mavedah on Sindie, there can be no war. And thus the Mavedah will have both peace and plenty." Uhe let the silence of impending death fall over it.

"Iyjiia, do you dispute my vision?"

The hunters gathered around the ring of masters more closely and looked at Iyjiia. The tips of the hunters' spears glinted in the light from the fire. The night was still, save for the relentless press of the death drums.

A servant of Aakva had a privileged position. Food, skins for the back, and skins to protect against cold and the wetness of night were provided by the tribe in exchange for the servant's studies and visions. To dispute Uhe's vision would mean ordeal by stoning or fire. Iyjiia liked its position. Iyjiia was old. And Iyjiia answered.

"I do not dispute your vision, Uhe."

The roar of approval from the gathered hunters was cut short as Bantumeh stood and shouted.

"*I* dispute your vision, Uhe!" Bantumeh turned toward Iyjiia. "May Aakva clean its waste with your cowardly mouth!" The ruler of the Mavedah faced Uhe. "I would see which of us Aakva favors with the stones!"

The challenge to ordeal was ended by the hiss of a hunter's spear sailing through the night. The pointed shaft entered Bantumeh's chest, and Bantumeh looked at it as though surprised. Up at the hunters went Bantumeh's eyes. "One has chosen for all."

And then Bantumeh fell.

Those who surrounded Bantumeh's still body felt the breath of Aakva's tabu against murder upon their necks. But no one looked to see who was missing its spear. And no one pulled the spear from Bantumeh's body to see whose sign the spear carried, until Uhe pulled the spear from the body and held it over its head.

"See you all that Aakva has spoken." And then Uhe threw the spear into the fire. If there were a sign upon the spear's shaft, it went to ash before their eyes. And it was whispered among the hunters that the shaft carried Aakva's own sign.

One hunter began the cheer, and then all the hunters cheered until their sound pushed the death drums from the night sky. All swore their obedience to Uhe and Aakva's new Law of War. The masters left the fire to convey Aakva's new law to their peoples, and the hunters there left to begin their preparations for the times to come.

As the beat of the death drums again filled the night air, Uhe was left alone at the fire, save for a hunter named Conseh who squatted next to the flames. Conseh's hands were clasped because it carried no spear. Conseh's face was impassive because it hid that which should not be known.

"Uhe, I have a question."

"Ask, Conseh."

And the hunter asked: "When Aakva talks to you, do you hear it through your head, your womb, or your belly?"

Uhe studied the hunter. It seemed to the servant that Aakva's tabus had taken ghostly forms and were dancing above the hunter's head.

"Conseh, you are impertinent."

The hunter stood and the images vanished. "I am not. My peace demands an answer. Aakva's new law speaks to most of us through the womb and belly."

"Do you dispute the new law, Conseh?"

The hunter waved its hands at the servant of Aakva. "I would not dispute you, for the God of the Day Light's new law speaks to all of us, and with a voice that cannot be silenced. But it is a law that any one of us could have made."

The servant of Aakva looked toward the fire. The shape of the murderer's spear was indistinguishable from the fire's sticks.

"I have no answer for you, Conseh."

Conseh looked toward the backs of its fellow hunters as they moved into the night to prepare for war.

"It is my wonder what the hunters will do once Aakva stops speaking to their wombs and bellies and begins again to speak to their heads."

The hunter left the fire. And to Uhe the hunter left both a question and a truth.

Joanne Nicole stopped the recording, and turned toward Vunseleh. It was wiping its hands. "Vunseleh, this Uhe is a savage. What is this savage doing in your *Talman:* your path of life?"

The Drac put away its medications, then stood silently for a long while. "Joanne Nicole, each Koda of *The Talman* has in it a number of truths. Through the events of the stories, those truths are revealed. It is for the student to find the truths that best serve its own talma." Vunseleh paused again. "For me, Uhe was the first one in my race's history to stand up and say, 'God is wrong!' Uhe did that, and then stood to bear the burden of its claim."

The footsteps walked from the room, Nicole replaced her robe, and continued listening to the story of the heartsick servant from the Madah—the poisoned land.

. . . As Uhe walked, it looked at the sky and addressed the light of the red clouds.

"Aakva, if you exist, and if you are God, why do you play with your creatures so?"

Uhe came among its warriors, and all cheered the demonstration of the truth of Uhe's vision of the new Law of War. . . .

"*. . . Why do you play with your creatures so?*"
Nicole stopped the story as she felt something twist within

her gut. Fear? No, it was a guilt that she could not identify.

How often have humans asked Uhe's question? When had I asked it last?

. . . Mallik's corpse on the litter; the dark brown faces of the fishers—their eyes offering sympathy, but demanding, in return, strength.

Strength for myself, and for Mallik's unborn child. . . .

Uhe was an ancient, alien creature. Hermaphrodite, superstition-ridden savage, and cannibal. Yet Nicole found Uhe touching something within her. She felt Uhe's desperation, its rage, its hope, its overwhelming guilt. But was Uhe driven by the plight of the Mavedah, or grief of the death of its child, Leuno? Did it matter?

Uhe's guilt was inflicted by an antiquated sun god. *Mine? I never did learn her . . . or his name. Its name.*

"You look unhappy, Joanne Nicole." The voice belonged to Vencha Eban.

"Vencha Eban, do you have any children?"

"No."

The Drac's voice reflected a sorrow of staggering depths. "After the birth of my only child, Hiurod, my reproductive organs . . . had to be removed. Hiurod died in the battle of Chadduk's Station."

"I am very sorry."

Vencha Eban was silent for a moment. "Joanne Nicole, do you have any children?"

She turned on her side and closed her eyes. "I don't want to talk anymore."

. . . *The cannibal of the Madah.*

Joanne Nicole was not aware of how many times she listened again to the Koda Ovida over the following days. But in her dreams she would see this Uhe and follow the ancient alien's bloody steps from the Madah through the lands that would be conquered and called Sindie.

And she would see Uhe as it stared at the old masters of the Mavedah as they picked over and gnawed on Leuno's bones—

—She would awaken; sometimes crying, sometimes screaming.

Then she would listen again to the story. While she listened, she would close her eyes and wait for her dreams to bring her, again, the sight of Uhe's face.

   . . . *And the face was not strange to her.*

8

And Maltak Di said to the student: "I have sixteen beads in my hand. If I give you six beads, how many beads will I have in my hand?"

"You will have ten, Jetah."

"Hold out your hand." And the student did so. Maltak Di then dropped six beads into the student's hand and opened its own hand to show that it was empty.

"You lied, Jetah!"

"Yes. Your response to my question should have been 'Jetah, open you hand and let me, first, see the sixteen beads.' Instead you answered from ignorance."

"Jetah, that is not fair!"

"Now you answer from stupidity."

—The Story of Maltak Di, Koda Nushada, *The Talman*

Nicole awakened but remained still, continuing to think upon the things she had seen in her dream. Uhe had denied the immortality of rules, had unleashed bloody war upon the Sindie to save the Mavedah, and had succeeded only to take its own life as payment in return for its guilt.

Uhe had placed the god, Aakva, aside; had declared to itself that the god was wrong; and had placed a stamp on the Sindie that continued down through almost twelve thousand years to the present.

V'Butaan on the planet Ditaar, named after the mountain city containing Uhe's tomb. The Tsien Denvedah, Uhe's front fighters of the same name, casting reluctant prisoners into the Madah. The terrorists on Amadeen taking on the venerable charge of the Mavedah, as well as its name.

And Joanne Nicole spoke Uhe's last words out loud: "Aakva, in the name of your children, become a more perfect god."

"A futile, but ancient, wish." The voice was deep, resonant, and just a touch amused.

Nicole sat up. "Who are you?"

There was a low chuckle. "Who am I? Who *am* I? Your question is profound, Joanne Nicole; and it would take me many hours to answer it. My name, however, is Tora Soam. I am the First Master of the Talman Kovah. It was my third child, Sin Vidak, that you saved from the fire on Ditaar."

"You have finally come, then?"

"Yes. Pur Sonaan told me that you had wondered at my absence; and for that I apologize. But you were near death for so long; and recently the demands upon my time have been heavy."

The voice was enigmatic; difficult to read. "Tora Soam, what is to become of me?"

"Ah, another profound question!" It paused for another chuckle. "But you refer to your immediate future, do you not?"

"Yes."

"The paths open to you would appear to be few. You are still vemadah, despite my protection." It paused for a moment. "There is a good argument, Joanne Nicole, that can be made supporting a claim to you being vehivida."

Vehivida? Of the sixth. And Uhe said: *"Their children will be sent to the Sixth Denve . . ."*

"I am not a child, Tora Soam."

"No, but you are infirm."

"I do not serve the Drac cause."

"Joanne Nicole, you served the cause by providing the Tsien Denvedah with another soldier."

She felt her face flush. "I saved a child; no more."

"Emmmm. You divide motive, act, and responsibility. Had you not saved my child, the child would not have become a soldier. Does not that, then, make you responsible for the existence of the soldier?"

Tora Soam's voice; it had an edge of humor in it. Tora Soam was playing games. "I saved a child. The child chose to become Tsien Denvedah."

"I see. And if you knew that the child would grow to become Tsien Denvedah, would you have refused to save it?"

"Drac, this game is getting quite tedious."

"Answer the question, Joanne Nicole. Would you have saved it, or would you have let it burn?"

Memories of that smoke-filled horror filled her mind. *All of those dead children, the heat, the smell.* She wiped her eyes as she shook her head. "I . . . I don't know."

"I think you do, Joanne Nicole."

Nicole smacked her hand upon her thigh. "All *right!* I would have saved it! But I was saving a life, not a soldier for the Dracon Chamber!"

Nicole heard the rustle of the Drac's robes as it stood up. "I apologize to you, Joanne Nicole. I did not mean to upset you. If you insist, you are vemadah."

"I insist!"

"Pur Sonaan has told me that, except for your vision, you will be well soon. As soon as you can leave the Chirn Kovah, I will have you brought to the Tora estate. The Madah is a social state, not a tract of land. You may stay at my home for as long as you wish—at least until you are fully recovered."

Nicole laughed and held her hands to her face. "My eyes. When will they be well?"

"Pur Sonaan is working hard on the problem—"

"Tora Soam, there are a great many USEF soldiers in the Madah right now."

"And?"

"While you would put me up in security, they will still be vemadah. I would rather count on them than on the charity of a Drac."

Tora Soam was silent for a moment, then Nicole felt it bend over the bed and pick up Pur Sonaan's player. A click, a whiz, then another click. The Drac played the player on her lap. "Learn an old lesson, Joanne Nicole."

She heard its footsteps leaving as the voice from the player filled the room.

• • •

It was the narration of Namndas, Shizumaat's senior at the Temple of Uhe.

. . . The days passed, and by the time two new classes were formed, and my charges occupied the south end of the Madah Wall, Ebneh stood before the class to hear their recitations of Aakva, Rhada, Daultha, and Uhe.

When all had completed their recitations, Ebneh held out its hands. "We call the Story of Uhe the *Koda Ovida;* and what is the first truth?"

There are, of course, many truths within the first *Koda*. The student's task is to draw from the story the greatest truth. The first student stood and spoke the accepted truth of the story: "That it is Aakva's law that the servants of Aakva will speak the true wishes of Aakva."

Ebneh nodded, pleased. "And do you all agree?"

All of the students nodded, except for Shizumaat. Shizumaat stared through the columns at Uhe's tomb until Ebneh called out. "Shizumaat, were you listening?"

Shizumaat's eyes turned toward Ebneh. "I was listening."

"Do you agree with this student's interpretation of the *Koda Ovida?*"

"No." Shizumaat looked back toward Uhe's tomb.

Ebneh stood next to Shizumaat. "You will stand!" Shizumaat stood and looked at Ebneh. "What truth do *you* see in the *Koda Ovida?*"

"Ebneh, I see that a rule stood between the Mavedah and survival; I see that the rule was nothing sacred, but made by Sindie; and I see that Uhe saw this and cast the rule aside to save its people. The truth I see, then, is that rules are meant to serve the Sindie; the Sindie is not meant to serve rules."

Ebneh stared at Shizumaat for a long moment; and then it asked: "Then, Shizumaat, should we, or should we not, obey the wishes of Aakva handed down by the servants?"

"If the rule is good, it should be used; if it is not good, it should be cast aside."

Ebneh's eyes narrowed, and those who sat near Shizumaat edged away. "Shizumaat, do you say that the laws of Aakva can be false?"

I closed my eyes. Ebneh was forcing Shizumaat into blasphemy. Shizumaat was smart enough to know this; it was too stubborn, however, to bow to the pain the servants would inflict on its body upon the admission of the blasphemy.

"Shizumaat spoke: "If the laws come from the servants, then the laws come from mortal, fallible creatures, and can be false."

Ebneh stood upright. "But if the laws come from Aakva?"

"Then Aakva can be and has been wrong. This I saw in the Story of Uhe."

A terrible silence came down upon the temple. I rushed up to Shizumaat and grabbed it by the arm. "Think, Shizumaat! Think upon what you say!"

Shizumaat pulled its arm away from my grasp. "I have thought upon it, Namndas. That is why I answered as I did."

Ebneh pushed me away from the student. "Do you know what you will suffer because of your words?"

Shizumaat smiled. "Yes, Ebneh. I know the rules."

"You know them, yet you scorn them?"

"I question them; I question their source; I question their validity. I know the servants will beat me for what I have said; but I ask you this: will beating me prove the existence of Aakva and the truth of its laws?"

Ebneh did not answer.

In the morning, with the Parent of All illuminating the eastern columns of the temple, I climbed the steps and found Shizumaat kneeling between the columns, facing Aakva.

Shizumaat's face rested against the paving stones. The the stones were stained with the deep yellow of the student's blood. Shizumaat's eyes were closed, its chest heaving. Behind Shizumaat were two servants holding whipping rods. Ebneh stood to Shizumaat's side and spoke: "Look up, Shizumaat. Look up!"

Shizumaat placed its hands upon the blood-stained stones and pushed until it sat back upon its heels, the morning light of Aakva showing the grey of Shizumaat's face.

"I am looking."

"What do you see?"

Shizumaat teetered for a moment, its eyes squinted, then it took a deep breath and exhaled slowly. "I see the great morning light we call Aakva."

Ebneh bent over and hissed into the student's ear. "And is that light a god?"

"I do not know. When you say 'god' . . . what do you mean?"

"God! God is god!" Ebneh grabbed Shizumaat's shoulder with one hand and pointed at Aakva with the other. "Is that the Parent of All?"

Shizumaat's shoulders slumped and it slowly shook its head. "I do not know."

"What does your back tell you, Shizumaat?"

"My back tells me many things, Ebneh. It tells me that you are displeased with me; it tells me that live meat whipped with sufficient enthusiasm will split and bleed; it tells me that the process is painful." Shizumaat looked up at Ebneh. "It does not tell me that Aakva is a god; it does not tell me that the laws of the servants are sacred truths."

Ebneh pointed at the two rod-carrying servants. "Lay into this one until its back *does* speak truth to it!"

One of the servants turned and walked into the temple. The other studied Shizumaat for a moment and then handed its rod to Ebneh. "Shizumaat's back has learned all that a rod can teach it. Perhaps you can think of a more persuasive argument." Then the second servant turned and went into the temple.

Ebneh stared after the departing servant, then threw away the rod and looked down at Shizumaat. "Why do you defy Aakva?"

"I do not. I only tell the truth that I see. Would you prefer that I lie to you? Would that serve your truth?"

Ebneh shook its head. "You will shame your parent."

"My parent's ignorance is not evidence of a god, Ebneh."

Shizumaat bowed its head until Ebneh turned and walked into the temple. Then Shizumaat looked up at me. "Namndas, help me to your room. I cannot make it by myself."

I pulled the student to its feet. "Do you not want me to take you to your own home?"

Shizumaat laughed. "A beating in defense of my understanding of truth is one thing, Namndas. I am not up to my parent beating me because I was beaten. That seems somehow to be taking the gesture past integrity into foolishness."

Shizumaat closed its eyes and slumped into my arms. I lifted it and carried the student from the temple to my room off the square—

Nicole turned off the player.

. . . Taking the gesture past integrity into foolishness.

She thought to herself: *Will I serve my purpose by not accepting Tora Soam's offer? Will I shorten the war? Will I do anything more than inflict an additional burden on vemadah such as Tokyo Rose? Am I being stubborn for the sake of some abstract—*

"Well?"

Nicole jumped at the sound of the voice. It was Tora Soam's. "I thought . . . you had gone."

"Obviously you were in error. What is your decision?"

Nicole thought for a moment, then nodded. "I will come to stay at your estate, Tora Soam."

"Emmmm. There is a saying—no one knows the author's name. But it observes that telling a human that his clothing is on fire takes a sharp stick, a large mirror, and a loud voice." Tora Soam paused for a moment. "It is just possible that the stick is unnecessary. Until you are well, then, Joanne Nicole."

Its footsteps left the doorway and faded down the corridor. Nicole sat silently for a moment, then punched at the player, continuing with a random portion of the Koda Nuvida.

That night, first I noticed that the temple lights had not all been raised to the proper height. Then I saw young Shizumaat, its face upraised, dancing in slow whorls upon Uhe's Tomb!

I rushed to the center of the temple and came to a stop with my hands upon the stone cover of the vault. "Shizumaat! Shizumaat, come down! Come down or I will execute you before the servants can get at you with their rods!"

Shizumaat stopped its dance and looked down at me. "Namndas, come up here and join me. I have the most wonderful thing to show you."

"You would have me dance upon Uhe's grave?"

"Come up here, Namndas."

Shizumaat returned to its whirling, and I grabbed the edge of the cover and pulled myself up, swearing to break Shizumaat into three hundred pieces. Once I stood, Shizumaat pointed toward the ceiling.

"Look up, Namndas."

The force in its words compelled me to look up, and what I saw was the disarray of temple lights. Their heights were arranged so that the lights were equally distant from a point just above the tomb, forming a hemisphere. And not all of the lamps were lit.

"Shizumaat, we will both be driven from the temple for this night's work."

"Don't you see it? Look up, Namndas! Don't you see it?"

"See what?"

"Dance, Namndas. Dance! Turn to your right."

I turned, saw the lights whirl about me, then I stopped and faced my charge. "Shizumaat! This only makes my head swim! We must climb down from—"

"Aaah!" Shizumaat jumped from the tomb and hit the stone floor, running toward the eastern wall. I jumped and ran after.

When I reached the great stairs, Shizumaat was standing far into the dark center of the city square. I ran down the stairs, across the square, and stopped in the center as I angrily grabbed Shizumaat's left arm. "I shall gladly take a rod and do the servants' work for them, you crazy—"

"Look up, Namndas! Curse your thick skull! Look up!"

Still holding onto its arm, I looked up. What I saw were Aakva's children arranged in a pattern similar to the pattern of the temple's lights, but tilted toward the blue light of The Child That Never Moves.

"You have reproduced the arrangement of the night sky."

"Yes—"

"But this will not save your skin, Shizu—"

Shizumaat pointed toward the speck of blue light. "Turn your face toward The Child That Never Moves. Then, Namndas, turn slowly to your right."

I did so. The implications of what I saw turned my legs to water, and I sat with a thump upon the packed soil of the square. I put out my hands and touched the unyielding soil. "It cannot be!"

Shizumaat squatted next to me. "Then you have seen it, too!"

I nodded. "Yes, I have seen it."

With the morning's light, the servants of Aakva found both of us dancing upon Uhe's tomb. . . .

9

We stood there, the mortar drying upon our hands, and Shizumaat pointed at the column of rocks we had built.

"You shall wait for me here, Namndas; at this mark. If I am correct, I shall see you again, and at this place."

I looked from the Akkujah out over the Madah, then back at Shizumaat. "And if you do not return? What then, Shizumaat?"

"Then either I am wrong about the shape of this world, or I did not have the strength to prove myself right."

"If you fail . . . If you fail, Shizumatt, what should I do?"

Shizumaat placed a hand upon my arm. "Poor Namndas. As always, it is your choice. You can forget me; you can forget the things we have learned; or you can attempt to prove that which I am attempting to prove."

—The Story of Shizumaat, Koda Nuvida, *The Talman*

Joanne Nicole's first shower. The water pierced her skin, making her feel as though she were in a high-velocity stream of needles. It hurt, but felt so good. Vunseleh, operating the controls, cut off the water. Slightly warm air, smelling of flowers, shot up from the floor.

"Turn in the air column, Joanne Nicole, and it will dry you."

She turned in the rush of sweet-smelling air, running her fingers through her hair to fan it. "Vunseleh, what is that smell?"

"Smell? Oh, there is a fine spray of oil in the air column. It is for aesthetic purposes, and it softens the skin."

"Is it safe . . . for me? I remember what happened with the burn ointment."

"It is safe. It has been used on humans many times with no ill effects."

The blower stopped and her hair was still wet. She felt her skin. It was not wet, but it felt slightly moist—pleasant. She could feel no scarring from the burns. "Do you have a towel?"

"A towel?"

"Something—a cloth—to dry my hair."

A hand touched her hair, then withdrew. "Emmmm. It is not good to keep you in the dry cycle until that mess is finished." Vunseleh's footsteps left the shower room then returned. Nicole felt a robe thrust into her hands. "Use this. I have another robe for you to wear." She threw the robe over her head and began drying her hair. "Joanne Nicole?"

"Yes, Vunseleh?"

"Is hair functional?"

Nicole paused for a moment, then continued rubbing the robe against her hair. "I suppose not. Why?"

"We could have it removed. It would make your cleansings more efficient; and less time consuming."

She held the wet robe out until the Drac took it, then used her fingers to again fan her hair. "Thank you, Vunseleh, but I think I'll keep it. Sentimental reasons."

It handed her another robe, and she began putting it on. "I have seen female humans with such hair before. Usually it is more . . . even."

Once her robe was on, Nicole felt her hair. On the right side of her head, the hair was short and ragged. "The fire, Vunseleh. My hair was burned in the fire. I could use a . . . I can't think of the word. My hair should be cut to make it even."

"Emmmm." Vunseleh took her hand and led her from the

shower stall. "We should be able to do that. Is anesthetic required?"

"No. It is a routine cosmetic task."

"Emmmm. I will see what can be done."

Nicole felt Vunseleh's hands open the front of her robe, then one of its hands cupped her left breast and squeezed it. She pulled back and tightened the robe around her. "What do you think you are doing?"

"Those things—you must look your best before being presented to the Ovjetah. Those things ruin the drape of the robe."

Joanne Nicole chuckled a bit nervously. "I don't know what you have in mind, Vunseleh, but these things stay put. Hands off, understand?"

"Perhaps they could be strapped down. They seem sufficiently malleable—"

"Forget it!"

There were many English words Joanne Nicole wished had equivalents in Dracon. "Just forget it, Vunseleh, understand?"

"If you wish."

"I wish."

Vunseleh led her back to her bed. She climbed upon it and turned to Vunseleh as she wound and draped the robe about herself.

"Is there anything else you need, Joanne Nicole?"

She thought for a moment. "Yes. Just who *is* Tora Soam? What is the Ovjetah of the Talman Kovah?"

There was a very long silence. Then Vunseleh spoke. "Considering your content of knowledge, I am not certain how I should answer." The Drac paused again. "How much of *The Talman* do you know?"

"I have listened to 'The Myth of Aakva,' 'The Story of Uhe,' and parts of 'The Story of Shizumaat.'"

"Emmmm. If I should tell you that Tora Soam is the most important being among the seventy-two planets of the Dracon Chamber, would you understand?"

"Tora Soam is your political or military leader?"

"No. Nothing of the sort."

"A kovah; I know what a school is. Is Tora Soam a teacher?"

"Of a sort—but more than that. Much more." Vunseleh was silent for a long time. "Joanne Nicole?"

"Yes?"

"Would you object to listening to the entire document of *The Talman?*"

"Why should I?"

"Your answers are there, if you have the wit to comprehend them. I shall send Vencha Eban to you with a pair of cutters. Tell Vencha what you want done with your hair."

Vunseleh's footsteps left the room. Nicole groped around upon her bed until she found the player. She indexed to the Koda Nuvida, "The Story of Shizumaat," and stretched out to listen.

> *Rhada said that God is;*
> *Uhe said that God is wrong;*
> *Shizumaat said that god is irrelevant....*

In the days that followed Joanne Nicole listened to *The Talman* several times. It was more than the history of a race. It was the story of the evolution and use of method: talma.

The word 'talma' had no equivalent in English. The word seemed to apply to anything composed of system: direction, ordered events, life, equation, methods, law, procedure, path, road, science, sanity.

In the period containing late human prehistory, Shizumaat intuitively came up with what is essentially the scientific method. Through its method, the young student derived its theory of worlds: the rotation and configuration of Sindie; that Aakva and its children were fires at varying distances; that the other stars could have about them bodies such as Sindie; and the concept of Universe.

To gather evidence in support of its theory, Shizumaat traveled the equator of the planet, leaving the faithful Namndas to wait at the monument the two of them had built. Many years later, after discovering many new oceans, lands, and peoples, Shizumaat appeared in the east and came to the monument.

At the return of Shizumaat, Namndas was ecstatic; but Shizumaat's mind was occupied with a new problem: understanding the method—talma—it had used to see what others could not.

Before Shizumaat's execution at the hands of the Servants of Aakva, it had communicated its conclusions to Namndas, who in turn taught these things to Vehya.

• • •

Vencha Eban was snipping away at her hair. "Joanne Nicole, did you not find Shizumaat's adventures exciting?"

Nicole thought for a moment. "Yes, but . . . do you see the greatness of the thing it did?"

"Which thing? Its struggle to cross the Madah? The crossing of the poisoned seas? Shizumaat outwitting the Hadyi, or its combat with Seuorka, Chief of the Omela?"

"I meant Shizumaat's discoveries: its theory of worlds; its discovery of talma?"

"But everyone knows that, Joanne Nicole."

Nicole felt slightly exasperated. "They know it now, because Shizumaat taught it then!"

The snipping stopped.

"I do not understand why you are angry."

"Vencha Eban, can you not see that Shizumaat's discovery of talma is more important than all of its other adventures combined?"

The snipping resumed for a moment, then stopped. "I do not fly or fight among the stars, Joanne Nicole. I clean floors."

The snipping continued.

In the Koda Ayvida, Vehya taught talma to Mistan, who used it both to improve talma, and to invent writing. Mistan's students reproduced the stories of Aakva, Uhe, and Shizumaat; and Shizumaat's talma spread throughout the world of the Sindie.

The Koda Schada told of the increasing oppression of the Servants of Aakva's rule, their overthrow by Kulubansu, and almost five hundred years after Shizumaat's birth, the story of Ioa, who founded the first Talman Kovah.

The Schada concluded with the invasion of the Sindie by the Hadyi, the destruction of the kovah and the dispersal of the Talmani, and the death of Lurrvanna under the rule of Rodaak The Barbarian. Then followed almost four hundred years of war as the different races of the planet Sindie struggled for dominance.

The Koda Itheda told of Aydan and the War of Ages. Aydan, a secret Talman Master, applied talma toward the task of waging war, then toward the task of establishing and maintaining peace. As the warring neared its end, another Talman Master, Tochalla, began the movement to reassemble the Talmani and to rebuild the Talman Kovah.

The following books of *The Talman* tell of the next six thousand years of progress and application of talma under many Jetai: Cohneret, Maltak Di, Lita, Faldaam, Zineru, Dalna.

Throughout this period, talma is made the core of a unified science of existence. By 2000 BC, the Sindie had made its first probes into space.

The Story of Dalna, in the Koda Siayvida, is the last of the Sindie books of *The Talman*.

Pur Sonaan visited to inform Nicole that the solution to her blindness was still outside its talma. "But I am constantly working to move the limits, Joanne Nicole."

"Pur Sonaan, you are called a Jetah, but of the Chirn Kovah."

"Yes."

"But you speak of talma the same as any Talmani."

"I am Talmani. I apply talma toward the goal of health."

"When I was an intelligence officer, I saw recordings of Drac prisoners. Soldiers; Tsien Denvedah. They, too, spoke of talma. One of them called itself a Jetah."

"The soldier and the health master are in the same discipline, Joanne Nicole. They specialize according to the goals they desire and the diseases that stand in the way of those goals."

The first of the Draco books, the Koda Sishada, tells first of the division of the Talmani. Almost two hundred years after the death of Dalna, it is proven that Sindie is a dying planet.

A movement begins within the Talmani to escape Sindie and find other planets upon which to live. The larger faction chooses to remain on Sindie, hoping for a solution; or as the ancient Mistan wrote in the Koda Ayvida: "Talma shows each one its path. But, as beings of choice, we can choose not to see the signs."

. . . Mitzak reading the news to her, and from all she could tell, the war was stalled; going badly for everyone. Military casualties were into the millions; civilian casualties were into the billions. . . .

"Mitzak, what are you going to do after I leave here?"

"My plans are made."

"Are you going back with the Drac Fleet?"

"No. Thanks to my service to Tora Soam, I am being allowed to continue my work at the Talman Kovah. I think I have had enough of this war...."

The Koda Shishada concluded with the Story of Atavu, the Ovjetah of the Talman Kovah, who left with the armada of generation ships toward the unknown. Two hundred and forty years later, Poma writes the Koda Sitheda. Poma is one of the founders of Draco and the Ovjetah of Draco's Talman Kovah. The stories of Eam, Namvaac, and Ditaar, the last three books of *The Talman*, tell of the development of Draco and the colonization of many other planets, and the beginning and end of the Thousand Year Rebellion, which saw the formation of the first Dracon Chamber more than a century before the birth of Copernicus.

Until the USE had come into conflict with the Dracon Chamber over the issue of the planet Amadeen, Dracs had seen nothing but hundreds of years of peace....

Talma.

Talma is composed of fundamental rules of situation assessment, goal definition, and goal achievement; methods for finding out where one is, where one wants to go, and how to get from the former to the latter; individually and/or collectively. It is the foundation for all activity, from individual conduct and social relationships to science, business, and law.

The Jetai, masters of the Talman, are the ones who study, invent, experiment with, and apply these fundamental rules. The Talman Kovah is their institution; as much laboratory as it is library and philosophers' hall. The Ovjetah is the First Master of the Talman Kovah. And Tora Soam was the current Ovjetah: the overseer of talma.

Tora Soam was the Drac equivalent of a chief economist, political theorist, attorney-general, first military strategist, the board of the USE Academy of Sciences—and too many other things—all rolled into one person.

And if the war ever paused long enough for a truce, Tora Soam or some subsequent Ovjetah would advise the negotiations for peace. And Nicole felt that peace would have to come, or there would be no human race. The Dracs had fought an interplanetary war for a thousand years without a moment of shaken resolve. Tokyo Rose had said that the war would not last forever. But the Dracs were prepared to fight for all of the forever that belonged to Joanne Nicole.

Then came the day she was to leave the Chirn Kovah.

On her feet were open sandals. Everyone who cared to had wished her well; and Pur Sonaan had promised to keep her informed of any progress in its research efforts. Pur had also added a cryptic sentiment:

"Joanne Nicole, if things go well in the future, you will have great cause to hate me. When that time comes, I ask you to remember this moment. The things I have done..." Pur searched for words. *"This I should not say. May the many mornings find you well."*

Nicole sat on the edge of her bed, feeling the softness of her new robe, slightly apprehensive about leaving the known of the room for the unknown on the other side of the walls.

There were strange footsteps. They halted and there was a moment of silence. "I am Tora Kia. I have been sent to bring you to my parent's estate."

She stood up. "My name is Joanne Nicole."

Hard footsteps crossed the room and a rough hand grasped her left arm. "We must go now."

There was the sharp odor of happy paste. Nicole reached for the arm that was holding hers and touched the cuff of a sleeve. Drac civilians wear robes.

"Who are you?"

"I said my name is Tora Kia. I am the firstborn of Tora Soam."

"This sleeve says you are wearing a military uniform."

"I am—was—Tsien Denvedah." There was a laugh; an almost hysterical laugh. "You will find the other sleeve empty, human."

10

And Lurrvanna looked up from its bandaged stumps and spoke to its students:

"Talma is forbidden to us. The Talman Kovah has been destroyed. Our friends have been either murdered or frightened into hiding. Our writings earn their authors the loss of their hands. Rodaak and its soldiers would have The Talman disappear from Sindie.

"But memory is the refuge of the Talmani, and it is there where we shall hide The Talman from Rodaak. Fix the words into your minds; then take them, whisper them to others, and have those others fix into their minds The Talman.

"The eternity of truth makes a friend of time. In time, Rodaak will no longer be. In time, we shall make known again the value of talma. In time, The Talman will again be written and the walls of the new Talman Kovah will stand upon these broken stones. In time, tomorrow will come."

—The Story of Ioa and Lurrvanna, Koda Schada,
The Talman

As Nicole was being hurried from the Chirn Kovah into Tora Kia's waiting vehicle, a strange thought crept into her mind:

95

she was curious about these creatures, and what would happen to her; but, if she could have seen, she would have been terrified. Terrified of everything.

The loathing fairly radiated from Tora Kia, but it could easily have been human hate. The strangeness—the alien unknown—of everything was made almost familiar because the images from her eyes were prevented from overpowering her other senses and her ability to think.

Nicole was seated upon plush upholstery, a door slammed, and she inhaled the eternal smell of new car. More doors slamming, a weight depressed the upholstery to her left, a whine, then a gentle pressure against her back as the vehicle accelerated. The sounds of other traffic came dimly through the vehicle's sound insulation.

Tora Kia barked out an order: "To the estate, Baadek."

"Your parent asked me to deliver these notes—"

"Then return to the city and deliver them—*after* you have delivered this . . . *guest* to the estate!"

Both of the other occupants of the vehicle remained silent as the sounds of traffic died and the change in pressure on Nicole's eardrums said that they were climbing in altitude. Still there were the sounds of the road. They were moving up into some mountains.

"You are silent, human."

"I didn't think, Tora Kia, that you would appreciate conversation coming from my direction."

"Dah!"

They rode in silence a moment longer.

"Tora Kia, your parent doesn't seem to carry your weight of hate."

"My parent! My parent has all of its limbs. To Tora Soam, the war is . . . an immense puzzle to be solved; a fascinating problem. I think my parent basks in the size and complexity of the puzzle. You and I are nothing more than two factors among the trillions that comprise this puzzle."

"You seem bitter."

"And they say that you are blind." Heavy sarcasm.

They seemed to go higher, the road twisting left and right. The silence in the compartment was oppressive. The sharp smell of happy paste again assaulted her nostrils and the one called Baadek spoke. "Kia, your parent—"

"Mind the road, Baadek! When Tora Soam has carried its

butcher ax against the enemy on Amadeen, then its views upon my medications will be of interest to me." The sharp smell remained in the compartment. "Ah, human. What an ugly thing you are."

"It would concern me more, Tora Kia, if I could see."

The Drac laughed, then that sharp smell grew sharper. "It is true. The war has treated us both badly, human. Was your life's work dependent upon your eyes? That is my sincere wish."

"Why?"

"I am looking for an equality of disaster."

"I've seen Drac soldiers with artificial limbs before. Those soldiers seemed to function adequately."

"Emmmm. True, it takes little skill to fry a human. But I am a musician, Joanne Nicole. The machine the Fleet will pay to have hammered onto this stump will find the strings of a tidna difficult to master."

The tidna: a kind of harp. "I am sorry."

"Sorrow is a cheap fee." A pause and more of that sharp smell. "Baadek! Stop here!"

"Tora Kia, your parent will have my skin for a cape if it should find out—"

"Stop here, you miserable fungus, or I will reach up there and pull off your head."

The vehicle slid to a stop and Nicole heard the door on Tora Kia's side open as a blast of icy air entered the compartment. The Drac's hand pulled at her left arm. "Come. Come with me, Joanne Nicole."

She slid across the seat and stepped out into ankle-deep snow. Tora Kia dragged her along until she had lost both of her sandals and stood barefoot.

"Baadek! Baadek, turn off the car!"

The whine of the car died, and on the gentle wind Nicole heard...music. Strange, haunting notes coming from below. "Down there, in the valley, Joanne Nicole. That was my kovah."

They listened for a time to the sounds. It felt as though knives were being thrust again and again through her feet. "Tora Kia, I am cold."

"The Universe is cold." The breeze brought her that sharp smell again. "My parent. You think it feels gratitude to you for pulling Sin Vidak from the oven?"

"That is what Tora Soam—"

Tora Kia's laugh seemed to be aimed at more than its words revealed. "Tora Soam feels *nothing!* The Ovjetah of the Talman Kovah would have you at the estate as an object of curiosity—experimentation. Sin Vidak—that is the excuse my parent uses to make housing you acceptable in the eyes of . . . *aaaah!*"

A strong hand slapped her face, sending her reeling into the snow. Geometric shapes flashed before her eyes as the snow covered and burned her face. As though it were far away, Nicole heard a door slam, then soft footsteps. A hand pulled at her right shoulder, lifting her face from the snow.

Nicole pushed the hand away, sat back upon her legs, and wiped the snow from her face. There were still the mournful sounds of music on the air as the one called Baadek spoke softly to her. "I ask you a favor, human. If you do it, I will always be in your debt." Baadek put its hands beneath her arms and lifted her to a standing position. Nicole's face still burned from the snow and the force of Kia's blow.

"What's the debt of a Drac worth?"

"Human, Tora Kia carries the Tora line. Its behavior here would shame its parent. I ask you to be silent about what Kia did."

Nicole waved a hand in what she thought to be the direction of the car. "First, get me out of the snow; second, find my sandals; third, I will think about it." Baadek began leading her toward the car and Nicole stopped dead in the snow. "But I will tell you one thing right now, Drac: if that child of a kiz hits me again, I will take off its remaining arm and stuff it down its throat!"

"There is nothing to fear from Kia now. Kia is asleep."

"My feet hurt. The cold."

Baadek moved to her right side, placed her arm around its neck, and lifted her. As it carried her, Baadek muttered, "The war. Everything has changed since the war."

Nicole was too weary to answer. She was placed into the car, the door slammed, then a second slam, and the car whined to life and moved down the twisting road. They rode for a long while, then Nicole heard Tora Kia move.

"Unh. You. Your robe is wet. Your face is red." That sharp smell again filled the compartment.

"Don't you remember? You hit me."

"I did?" That smell grew stronger, then the voice became

very quiet. "I wish I had killed you."

And then Nicole found out something she never knew before: Dracs snore. "Baadek?"

"Yes, human?"

"My name is Nicole. Joanne Nicole."

"Yes, Joanne Nicole?"

"Why is Tora Kia hitting that drug?"

"Many of the Tsien Denvedah that fought on Amadeen have the same habit. Tora Soam disapproves."

Nicole pulled her legs up upon the seat and rubbed her feet. She felt warm air being directed upon them, and in moments they were dry. "Thank you, Baadek."

"When we get to the estate, we will stop at the gate house and I will get you a dry robe to wear."

She continued rubbing her feet. "Baadek, what is it to you if Tora Soam finds out that its child chews happy paste."

There was a long silence from the front of the car. "Nothing, I suppose. I have spent my life serving the Tora estate, probably from habit. Habit is very safe. The war soils everything, however. Perhaps I should change my habit, too."

Nicole's weight was thrown from one side of the car to the other as her stomach evidenced a sickening skid, the whine of the car's motor rising and falling in rapid succession. "It is only a guess, Baadek; but are you driving too fast?"

The motion of the car slowed as the whine from the motor decreased. "Yes.... Thank you. And my apologies."

She leaned her head against the back of the seat. *Baadek, the long-suffering family retainer coming home to its master hauling a drug-blitzed child and a backseat driver.* Nicole yawned from the drying heat blowing on her legs. *Perhaps I could take some of the weight from Baadek's already over-burdened shoulders.* "Baadek?"

"Yes, Joanne Nicole?"

"I will say nothing to Tora Soam concerning what happened today."

"Thank you. I will remember this."

"How much longer will we be riding?"

"We are almost a third of the way to the estate."

The warm air and sleep tugged at her. She moved her shoulders into the upholstered corner between the door and seat, her face leaned against something soft to her left. Vaguely she felt the gentle rocking of the car....

• • •

. . .Happy paste.

There had been reports that a large percentage of USEF personnel coming back from Amadeen had the habit.

How long had it taken Ted Makai to kick it? He never did, really. He just substituted other things.

. . .In the Storm Mountain officers club that time, Ted at the bar tossing down doubles. He was an island of dead gloom in a sea of laughter, trying to numb the nervous system that made him a rare exception among the Universe's life forms.

He ordered another.

"Ted, aren't you nailing those things down pretty fast?"

He never looked up; simply waited until his fresh drink came. He took the glass, tossed down its contents, and ordered another. He looked at her.

"Do your tour on Amadeen, Major Nicole, and then come back to me and preach temperance. . . ."

". . .When Tora Soam has carried its butcher ax against the enemy on Amadeen, then its views upon my medications will be of interest. . . ."

Amadeen. So little of the war had taken place there; but so much of the war owed its existence to the planet. . . .

. . .In the Chirn Kovah, searching for her reasons for fighting, a voice from nowhere reciting history. . . .

". . .The planet Amadeen was colonized in a succession of immigrations by both humans and Dracs, attracted there by Amadeen's vast mineral resources. Numerous private companies based in both spheres of influence were involved in the colonization effort, the two largest being the human Earth IMPEX and the Dracon JACHE companies.

"Although Timan Nisak, headquartered on the Planet Timan, is the third largest capital investor in Amadeen, there have been no Timanese immigrants. Timan Nisak operates the orbiting ore-processing station used before the opening of hostilities by all the mining companies operating on Amadeen.

". . .After the defeat of the Drac and human Centralist Party, extremist factions took control of the political mechanisms of both races. The Amadeen Front was the political party dominating the humans, while the Ka Mavedah rose to become the most influential political organization in the Drac-controlled areas of the planet. The Centralists of both races were effectively eliminated as political forces, and terrorist raids began. . . ."

Terrorism on Amadeen. Its victims and witnesses never seemed to talk about it much. The horrors were beyond comprehension. Humans were found still alive, their skeletons shattered with sound waves. The bones had been gone over one at a time. Dracs were found, their bellies ripped open, still living fetuses dangling from their umbilicals—

"Joanne Nicole?"

She awakened, warm air entering the car from her side. The door was open. "Baadek?"

"Yes. Here is your dry robe, and I have dried your sandals."

She leaned forward and took the robe and sandals. "Where can I change?"

"Here in the car will do."

"Where can I be *alone* to change?"

"Alone? . . . For what reason?"

"Because I *want* to be alone when I change."

A puzzled silence. "I suppose you may use the gate house." Nicole felt the Drac's hand touch her arm. "Come with me."

"What are you going to do with Kia?"

Baadek helped her from the car, her feet touching soft grass, warm sunlight washing her face. Baadek sighed.

"What to do with Kia? That is always a good question, Joanne Nicole. Always a good question. Come this way."

Nicole had been whisked up a huge outdoor staircase, then through a dizzying complex of halls and passageways. Each door seemed to have a guard on it with which Baadek would exchange hushed whispers. Then they were in a room that was bright with sunlight; she could feel it upon her skin. There were many low voices in the room, then one of the voices became recognizable; it was Tora Soam's.

"Here you are, at last, Joanne Nicole."

She nodded, her ears straining for every sound as the Ovjetah spoke to Baadek: "And where is Kia?"

"In its apartments, Ovjetah. Kia was not feeling well."

Tora Soam's silence spoke volumes. "Joanne Nicole, I hope your trip from the Chirn Kovah was satisfactory?"

"It was a learning experience."

"Emmmm." She heard Tora Soam turn away. "My colleagues, this is the human, Joanne Nicole." There was an uncomfortable period of coughing, paper rattling, and chair squeaking. "Baadek, come with me." Tora Soam took Nicole's arm and led her from the room. "Joanne Nicole, I apologize for my colleagues. However, please understand that you are the very first human as flesh that they have ever seen."

"I understand."

"Tonight I will have a surprise for you; until then, Baadek will show you your apartments. There are only a few places on the estate that you are not allowed to enter, and the guards at those places will prevent your entrance. Otherwise you have the freedom of the estate. Baadek will act as your eyes for the time being, and it will call for you at the night repast. I would like to have you join us for the repast."

Nicole nodded. "I will be there."

"Excellent. And now I must return to work." She heard Tora Soam's voice change direction. "Baadek?"

"Yes, Ovjetah?"

"When Kia is quite recovered, send my child to me. I shall be in the library all evening."

"Yes, Ovjetah."

Tora Soam's footsteps faded away and Baadek took Nicole's arm and led her through a maze of corridors. As they were walking, Nicole let the fingers of her left hand trail along the wall's cut stone surface, trying to place and memorize all of the twists and turns. "Baadek?"

"Yes, Joanne Nicole?"

"Why is this building made of cut stone?"

"It must have been the desire of Tora Kia—the founder, Kia; not the one you know."

"This building is as old as the founding of Draco?"

"Yes; almost. It is a very beautiful building. The stone is of many kinds and colors."

Nicole thought for a moment as they walked down still another corridor. "Baadek, why would a race that can use metals, plastics, and freeform masonry put up a mansion of quarried stone?"

Baadek walked in silence for a moment then pulled her to a stop. "I have searched your words for a meaning beyond the apparent, Joanne Nicole, but I can find no such meaning. Do you truly find it difficult to understand?"

"Yes. The time, the expense that must have been involved hardly seems rational with the construction alternatives that must have been available."

"I repeat, Joanne Nicole: it is a very beautiful building." Baadek leaned away from her and she heard a door open. "This is the entrance to your apartments."

11

After taking her on a tour of the greeting, entertainment, toilet, bathing, sleeping, and meditation rooms, Baadek left Nicole to her own devices until the night repast. As it was taking its leave, Baadek again thanked her for not reporting Kia's behavior to Tora Soam.

With some difficulty, she bathed and rested. When she

reached for her robe, she found another in its place. The fabric was as light and smooth as cobwebs; and when she placed it on it felt as though a warm, gentle film caressed her body. Instead of the open sandals, there were soft, lined slipper-boots. Tora Soam's castle might have been beautiful, but it was chilly. Joanne Nicole gathered that the Toras dressed accordingly.

While she waited for Baadek's call to dinner, she walked the walls of her apartments, beginning the task of memorizing the floorplan and the placement of each piece of furniture.

The apartment was a circle divided up into six equal segments—each segment being a room that opened onto a central circular accessway. Each segment was shaped like an orange slice truncated on both ends. The only flat surface was the floor. The center of each room contained the article or articles that served the room's name. The central accessway had six doors that could be opened in any combination.

There were some enigmatic Drac phrases that began to make some sense. "Greeted with all doors open" and "Greeted with all doors closed" described the degree of trust and intimacy a host extends to a visitor. The greeting room was bare, providing nothing more than a place to stand and talk. The entertainment room had deep, soft chairs and couches. The central door of the greeting room, and the door to the entertainment room being open was an invitation for a longer stay. A still longer stay was invited by the toilet room being open. Bathing, sleeping, and meditation rooms being open described more intimate invitations about which she could only speculate.

After her initial inspection, she entered the meditation room, closed the door, and settled on the cushions in the center of the room to await the call to the night repast.

She had been sitting for a few minutes, quietly trying to relax, when the room seemed to fill with a dim green light marbled with blacks and lighter greens. Her hands immediately went to her eyes, but her hands could not block out the light. The light was inside her head.

Again she relaxed and allowed the lights to move at random. There was a slightly drugged feeling, then a feeling of all-encompassing calm. One-by-one she could feel tense muscles relax, her body going limp. . . .

. . . There were the happy moments with Mallik, seen through a lens that would admit no pain. She opened to it and her being was flooded with love.

And their child swelling in her abdomen.

Mallik's head against the swelling, listening.

"You can't hear anything yet, Mallik; it's too soon."

His head burrowed his ear more deeply into her abdomen while his hand stole between her legs.

"If this is Mallik Nicole's child, it will be an early riser."

She laughed as she reached down to touch his face....

... There was a moment at Storm Mountain; a moment of love, pride, fierce unshackled joy.

Death covered the slopes, but the Tsien Denvedah was falling back. Her command hadn't a prayer of getting relief; they knew that another attack was coming that would crush them; they knew that most of them would be dead before the next two hours elapsed—

—but the Tsien Denvedah was *falling back.*

The hoots and catcalls started in the emplacements to her left. In seconds all of Storm Mountain was shouting insults at the retreating Dracs; her own voice joining the tumult.

The Tsien Denvedah was falling back!

It was another—a stronger—form of love than that between a man and woman. They were a blood and mud spattered brotherhood that had met the enemy and had turned them back. They had been dipped in fire and had survived to see the Drac Infantry pulling back.

Morio Taiseido collapsed beside her, his voice hoarse.

"Major, I could die content at this moment. We whipped them! Holy son of a bitch, we whipped them!"

... The lights came back and part of Joanne Nicole's brain asked another part if this joy was the appeal to battle; to war. If it was the truth, it would be an impossible motivation to treat rationally.

The rules were out; the ultimate consequences were out; nothing was in mind except the fact that the Dracs were falling back. In that minuscule particle of time, they were victorious....

... And then, as though it were being played before her upon a stage, she remembered The Story of Lita in the Koda Ovsinda.

Lita had invented a game for the students to play.

One of the students was selected by chance to begin the game, and its first move was to invent the first three rules of the game. And the game—the rules—could be anything.

The next player could proceed according to those first three rules, or could invent another rule. The rules and rule changes were never communicated except by the nature of the play. The rules and rule changes must be deduced from the actions of those who invented the rules. Even that which constituted "winning" changed from one minute to the next.

The most successful tactic was to understand all of the rules up until your turn, and then invent a rule or criterion of winning that negated the regulatory advantages invented by the previous players.

By the time the play came around to Lita, there was an impossible tangle of rules, stated, implied, most of them invisible. And then Lita would win the game by stating:

"I win."

A student would always protest. *"Jetah, you cannot win. The structure of rules that has been built does not allow it."*

"It most certainly does allow it. The rule I have invented is that when the play comes to my turn, I win."

"But, Jetah, the first player could have done the same. Any of us could have done it."

"Yes, but I did it first."

The green lights in her head died and became a warm, soft blackness. And there was a voice. It was Baadek's. "Joanne Nicole, it is time for the night repast."

She sat in wonder for a moment at the things she had seen. She stood up, made her way to the meditation room door, and opened it. "Baadek?"

"I am here." The voice was very close. "When you use the meditation room in the future, should you not want to be disturbed, close the outside entrance to your apartment."

"Thank you. What is in the meditation room that allowed me to see the things that I saw?"

"Only your own mind. The design of the room is an ancient one, conducive to looking at oneself."

"The lights, the green lights were so real."

"Usually the lights are blue—for Dracs."

Nicole began feeling her way toward the corridor, but Baadek's hand stopped her. "What is the matter, Baadek?"

"Understand, Joanne Nicole, that I have no love for humans."

"Who asked you to?"

There was a brief silence. "As an individual, I feel an obligation toward you. Be very careful at the night repast. Tora Soam's guests tonight include five Talman masters and a human. I cannot even guess at their roles, nor yours."

"Baadek, why this warning from one who has no love for humans?"

For just a moment, the Drac seemed to laugh. "I am no student of convoluted rules and gaming, Joanne Nicole. I am a simple creature of loyalty. Because of my loyalty to the Tora estate, I look upon myself as the protector of Tora Kia. Tora Kia has my loyalty. Because of your cooperation in this protection, my loyalty is extended to you as well—to a degree."

She paused. "Baadek, I appreciate your warning, but I do not understand. What are you warning me about?"

"It is hard for me to see. But I would not want you to betray yourself—the things that you value. I think that tonight you will be in an excellent position to do just that."

After walking the many twists and turns of the corridors, Baadek and Nicole entered a series of connected chambers that were sufficiently large that their footsteps and words caused echoes. It was in one of those chambers that she heard voices and smelled rich cooking. It was there that Tora Soam met them.

"Does the night find you well, Joanne Nicole?"

"Yes, it does."

"Excellent." Tora Soam paused and Nicole heard its robes move. "And, as I promised you, here is your surprise."

More footsteps. "Hi, Major."

"Benbo?" Nicole reached out her hands. "Benbo?"

"Right here, Major." A pair of hands touched her shoulders.

Some great knotted thing inside of her dissolved, making her legs limp. Benbo quickly grabbed her arms to keep her from falling to the stone floor.

Tora Soam's voice came very close, an edge of concern in it. "Joanne Nicole, are you ill?" Its voice changed direction. "She is just released from the Chirn Kovah."

Benbo spoke. "I think she is well, Ovjetah. It is just that

we have gone through much together, and that it has been a long time since we met last."

"How are you? Damn it, Benbo, how in the hell are you?"

"Fine, Major. Just fine."

The direction of his voice changed. "Ovjetah, she will recover in a moment. May we be alone?"

"Certainly, Amos Benbo. Please use those couches over there." Benbo led her across the chamber and lowered her into a deep, soft couch. She felt him sit on the couch beside her. Again Tora Soam spoke: "Joanne Nicole, the next part of your surprise waits with my other guests. He is Leonid Mitzak."

"Mitzak. It sounds like old home week."

"I . . . am not certain I understand; but would you like me to send him out here?"

"No, Tora Soam. I would like to be alone with Benbo for a while. Can you have Baadek call us when the repast is ready?"

"Of course. Until then. Come, Baadek."

Their footsteps left the chamber. She turned toward Benbo. "Amos, why are you here?"

Benbo laughed. "It sure beats the hell out of me. When I was snagged on Ditaar, I was busy making like a firebug. Right now, I am the special guest of Ovjetah Tora Soam, the grand poobah hisself—itself." His voice became very quiet. "Major . . . your eyes . . ."

Nicole shook her head. "I'm temporarily blind. It's all right. What happened to you after the attack?"

"I put you in a safe place—or thought I did—then I ran back to the V'Butaan field to check up on the troops. Do you know about them?"

She nodded. "Mitzak told me."

"Major, what in hell is going on here?"

"I don't know. I've been the ward of Tora Soam since V'Butaan, from all I can tell. What that means, or why it's so, I don't know. What about you?"

"I was picked up, brought here, and dropped by a couple of characters that it didn't look too smart to argue with. Beyond that, I don't know."

Baadek's voice called from a distance. "The night repast is prepared and ready. Will you join the company?"

Nicole pushed herself up from the couch. "Thank you, Baadek. We will be there in a moment."

Benbo was standing, and Nicole pulled him close and whispered, "You wanted to know what's going on here. I don't know, but I've been warned about this dinner party. You keep your trap shut unless you are asked a direct question, and then be very careful how you answer. Tora Soam's Drac guests are all Talman Masters—" The hint of a thought crossed Nicole's mind. Flowers. The slight odor of flowers.

"What is it, Major?"

Nicole shook her head. "Nothing. Just remember that every word you speak gives information to them."

Nicole was seated on one part of a long circular couch; Benbo to her right. On Benbo's other side sat Leonid Mitzak. Far to her right sat Tora Soam, and directly across from her were the five Talman Masters. In the center of the couch arrangement were the dishes of food. Tora Soam began the ritual: "This is the bitter weed we eat to remember the Madah. Never shall we return."

Nicole heard the Talman Masters take up grain from the center table, and then replace it. Tora Soam continued: "For the second repast, we eat fruit and say: 'This is the fruit of the Irrveden, for which the Mavedah fought.'"

Everyone picked up the strange bulbs and tubers that the Dracs called fruit. Benbo handed Nicole hers, and her jaws ached as her eyes watered at the acid taste of the raw plant. "For the third repast, we eat nothing, for this is the legacy of Mijii who burned its people rather than submit to the rule of the Mavedah."

She touched nothing to her tongue, but the smell of charcoal was heavy in the air. "The fourth repast—the night repast—celebrates Uhe's victory and the unification of the Sindie. This is the night repast; let us celebrate."

And then the food flowed. Strange meats, salads, ices, and cheeses passed her lips until her stomach sent up its all-full warning. Shortly after, the sounds of eating quieted, and she could hear the table being cleared. Benbo placed a hot mug into her right hand. "Here, Major. It tasts sort of like hot rubber soaked in dirty underwear."

She sipped at the brew as Baadek performed the peculiarities of introducing the guests to the host. Of course, Tora Soam knew all of those at the table. The introductions were more for the benefit of the guests. Baadek would move behind the person being described.

"Ovjetah, this guest at the table is Jetah Zigh Caida, First Deputy of the Dracon Chamber." Baadek moved behind the next guest: "Ovjetah, this guest..."

The Drac side of the table was rank-heavy. Besides the first deputy of the Chamber, Draco's governing body, there were: Raga Gia, Drac Fleet liaison officer to the Chamber; Xalta Lov, Nujetah, second master, of the Talman Kovah; Suinat Piva, Ovjetah of the Fangen Kovah, the school of social goal formulation; and Vikava Minose, liaison officer to the Chamber of the Denve Irkmaan—department of humans.

Baadek stood behind Mitzak. "Ovjetah, this guest at the table is Leonid Mitzak, student of the Talman Kovah." Footsteps. "Ovjetah, this guest at the table is Amos Benbo, vemadah." Baadek stood behind her. "Ovjetah, this guest at the table is Joanne Nicole, vemadah."

Tora Soam opened the talk: "Fellow masters, I see your puzzled expressions at having humans at the repast. I shall explain. As Ovjetah of the Fangen Kovah, Suinat Piva has known for some time that the facilities of the Talman Kovah have projected an armed truce with the forces of the United States of Earth."

There was excited chatter among the Dracs. A deep, old-sounding voice interrupted the chatter. "Soam, how far has the projection been substantiated?"

"It has been substantiated to the full capabilities of the kovah, Deputy Zigh."

Zigh Caida hissed. "This is of crucial importance. Why has not the Dracon Chamber been informed of this development?"

"It just has—wait." The grumbling from the Drac brass quieted down and Tora Soam continued. "There are several things upon which the occurrence and successful exploitation of this projected truce depend. The truce will follow immediately after a battle of certain configurations. This is a tactical matter, and the configurations will soon be made available to the Chamber and to the Dracon Fleet."

A voice spoke: "What has this to do with these humans, Soam?"

"Vikava Minose, you direct the Denve Irkmann."

"And?"

"And have you ever talked with a human?"

A pause. "No. But what of it?"

Tora Soam paused. "The truce is a thing that can last only

a moment and then lead to continued fighting; or it can lead to peace. Following the truce, Dracs and humans will gather to sort out and resolve the issues of the conflict. They will talk. The Talman Kovah has projected that you five, or your replacements, will probably be those who will represent the Dracon Chamber at the talks, provided that the battle mentioned takes place within the next eighty days."

The voice of Vikova Minose spoke: "Ovjetah, an enemy is an enemy. You were to speak to why these . . . humans are at your table."

Tora Soam answered, its voice slow and thoughtful. "When you face the humans, you will have in your hands the ability to bring this war to an end. You will also have the ability to throw three hundred worlds—Drac and human—back into war."

Deputy Zigh Caida spoke: "Soam, what does this have to do with your . . . *other* guests?"

"It is simple, Deputy Zigh: if there is to be peace, or if there is to be more war, sense dictates that talma is best followed if the result is a matter of studied choice rather than a matter of ignorance, anger, or accident. One does not need to take to diagrams to see the truth in this. If all of you have at least some experience with human thinking, the chances of the negotiations being conducted and settled on an intelligent basis are improved—"

"Wait!" The voice was Tora Kia's.

"My guests, this is Tora Kia, my firstborn. Why do you interrupt, Kia?"

Footsteps entered the room. "Ah, my parent, in your game you have overlooked the two most important parties to the negotiations. Where is the Mavedah? Where is the Amadeen Front?"

Raga Gia snorted out a scornful laugh. "I refuse to have the Front at the talks." Its voice changed direction. "Does this comply with your game, Soam?" Raga's voice turned again in Kia's direction. "The United States of Earth will represent the interests of the Front, and the Dracon Chamber will represent the interests of the Mavedah."

Tora Kia laughed. "No, no, my parent's most respected guest. The interests of the Dracon Chamber are not identical to those of the Mavedah."

Sergeant Benbo spoke for the first time. "Raga Gia, if the Front is no part of the negotiations, there can be no peace. If negotiations ever happen, the Amadeen Front will want its own representative. The Front only wants an end to the war under certain terms. It is the same with the Mavedah."

The direction of Tora Kia's voice changed. "Human, how are you called?"

"Amos Benbo."

"Have you done your time upon Amadeen, Amos Benbo?"

"Yes. And you?"

"Yes."

Zigh Caida spoke: "Kia and this human speak the truth, Soam. There will be four sides at the negotiations. I propose that we enlist Tora Kia to represent the Mavedah, and Amos Benbo to represent the Amadeen Front."

Nicole heard Mitzak stand. His voice sounded deeply troubled. "Ovjetah, I do not wish to participate in this game. I am a student at the Talman Kovah. Therefore, my loyalties, as well as my method of thinking, would corrupt my performance as a human."

"You *are* a human, Mitzak." Tora Soam's voice was deadly. "Whatever your views or methods of thinking, the first thing the Drac negotiators must overcome is the sight of your face." She heard Mitzak sit down. "Very well, Deputy Zigh, we now have four parties to this session. Who shall begin?"

"Ah, games such as this would best be left inside the walls of the Kovah," Zigh grumped. "Very well, each side should formulate its goals—what it hopes to achieve from the negotiations. Once we have all seen the diagrams—"

Nicole spoke: "There will be no diagrams, First Deputy. Human negotiators are not familiar with talma."

"Surely there must be a human equivalent?"

"Situation assessment, goal formulation, and path construction and evaluation are not systemized disciplines among humans."

Exasperated wheezing seemed to come from First Deputy Zigh's direction. The wheezing paused. "Goals must be stated in *some* manner!"

Mitzak laughed. "Yes, they will be stated with force, bombast, and fine-sounding subjective phrases that cannot be taken literally. Their true goals must be deduced from the fog of words they will spread in front of you, and from their actions, which will probably contradict what little true meaning their words might contain."

There was disturbed silence from the Drac side of the table until Ovjetah Suinat Piva of the Fangen Kovah burst out in laughter. "I see your game, Tora Soam. Very clever, and you have my compliments."

"My thanks, Piva. May we continue?"

"Of course. Let us say that since Amadeen is the root of this war, we should hear first from the Front and the Mavedah."

Nicole felt Benbo stand up. "I think I can save some time here. The positions of the Mavedah and the Front are similar. The Front won't be satisfied until every last Drac on Amadeen is either dead or removed from the planet." He sat down.

Tora Kia spoke. "And the Mavedah will settle for nothing less than the human population on Amadeen being either dead or removed. How much room, Tora Soam, does that leave you for problem solving?"

"Apparently none, Kia. However, I think you already can see the error in depending upon the apparent for your answers. Joanne Nicole, would you state the position of the United States of Earth?"

She rubbed her temples and let the stories of *The Talman* race through her mind. So much of talma involved goal choices; fitting the desired within the possible. She could not separate the formulas in her mind. "I would hear, first, the position of the Dracon Chamber."

A murmur of approval came from the Dracs. Then Zigh Caida spoke. "In gross phrases, then, we would see an end to the fighting—at least a confinement of the fighting to the immediate area of Amadeen. The Drac Fleet would stand armed, as would the USE forces. But there would be no fighting."

"A cease-fire?"

"Yes."

Nicole thought upon Zigh Caida's words. "If war could continue upon Amadeen without our two sides fighting, why is there fighting now? The truce must include a truce upon Amadeen. A separation of the combatants by a policed, demilitarized zone."

Zigh Caida asked, "And, Joanne Nicole, who shall have the responsibility for policing this zone?"

"A third party we could both agree upon; or a joint Drac-human force."

"Emmmm. This is . . . agreeable; but it does not solve the problem upon Amadeen. Amos Benbo?"

"Yes?"

"If we could establish a truce with a demilitarized zone in the manner described by Joanne Nicole, what would the Front's position be?"

"No change. The Front won't put down its weapons until every last Drac on Amadeen is dead."

"What of the demilitarized zone?"

"What of it?"

Nicole shook Benbo's arm. "Amos, quit fooling around."

She could feel the rock-hardness of Benbo's muscles. "I am not joking. Tora Kia knows that I am not joking."

Zigh Caida's voice changed direction. "Tora Kia?"

"The human speaks the truth. The Mavedah has many old scores to settle. The Mavedah can settle for nothing less than Amadeen free of human life."

Tora Soam spoke. "Amos Benbo, your position does not allow the machinations of talma to work. There must be at least some degree of flexibility on your part; otherwise there can be no resolution."

"Let the Mavedah be flexible."

Tora Kia laughed. "My parent, you are more blind than Joanne Nicole. Can you not see that the Front and the Mavedah are way beyond rules? Beyond talma? They are beyond ultimate objectives. They are even beyond what will ultimately serve their own best interests. The Mavedah wants the Front dead; the Front wants the Mavedah dead."

"That serves nothing, Kia."

"My parent, until you have put in your time upon Amadeen, you have no idea what such position serves. But I will tell you what such a position serves. It serves death. On Amadeen, death must be served."

Nicole heard Kia's footsteps move from the room. Later, Benbo talked to Tora Soam, saying much the same things said by Tora Kia. But while he talked, Nicole remembered that moment upon Storm Mountain when the Tsien Denvedah was falling back.

The universe was extremely small at that moment. There were absolutely no considerations beyond the fact that the Dracs were falling back. Cooler heads would have seen that any resistance at that point was futile. But on Catvishnu, there were no cooler heads. No one was thinking about anything other than scoring against the Dracs, and to hell with other considerations.

Tora Soam spoke, and its words filtered through her growing headache. "Joanne Nicole, do you have a comment?"

She stood. "I would return to my apartments. Tora Soam?"

"Yes?"

"Your game has failed. And it is not because any one of us wanted it to fail. It failed because it had to fail. If a truce should happen, it will die as it has to die. The war, then, will resume. Before there is any solution, much more blood must be spent." Nicole held out her hand. "Baadek. Baadek!"

A Drac hand enclosed hers. "Yes?"

"Take me to my apartments. I have had enough of this foolishness."

12

*"Without a key, a door is a wall. Without a door, a
key is but matter. A door with a key in the presence of
mind is an opening. Without mind, neither the key, the
door, nor the opening can exist."*
　　—The Story of Lita, Koda Ovsinda, *The Talman*

That night she awakened; the edges of some dream-sired horror
still touching her; Mallik's name still on her lips. There was a
sound from the corridor—boots moving against the stone floor;
then the boots moving slowly away. On her bed with all doors
closed, Nicole breathed easily and allowed her thoughts to
move at their own initiative. And as Eam's thoughts spoke to
it of the eventual end of life upon the planet Sindie, Nicole's
thoughts spoke to her.

There was a fierce, lonely ache in her body. When she
recognized that the ache was for Mallik, she shut it off. Other
things . . . there were other things to think about.

Tora Soam's dinner party game. It had been a disaster. A
human of similar rank, entertaining a roomful of equivalent
human brass, would have been mortified. The guests would
have been mortified as well. But as Baadek was leading her
away, Nicole could hear the Dracs renewing the conversation

in amiable, unconcerned voices.

They were discussing the game, the *game*, much as, in the past, Nicole had seen humans chewing over a bridge or poker hand that had been completed. That was some sort of danger signal to her, because they were not humans; and they were not playing games.

But the . . . alienness of those creatures is the thing that keeps escaping me. They could be human.

Baadek had left Nicole at her door to return to the corridor and drive Benbo and Mitzak to their quarters. She would have liked to have talked with them more; but when she wanted the peace of her apartments, she reached out and called for Baadek.

Why?

She sat up and rubbed her eyes. Ever since her lights had been extinguished, she had been categorizing her experiences with the Dracs into analogs with humans.

Vencha Eban, the Drac who cleaned the floors at the Chirn Kovah. It made no difference that it was a Drac and that I knew it was a Drac; I always think of Vencha as "the cleaning lady." Eban is a simple, hardworking, "Maggie the Mop."

Baadek, the long-suffering family retainer. In my mind Baadek is every bit the comedic representation of the ex-slave running down the dirt road, tears in his eyes, blubbering his welcome as massa done come home fum de wawh.

"Dammit, and what is Tora Soam?"

The darkness around her absorbed the question, letting her see the answer. Mallik's father, Eliem Nicole. Ever since she could remember, Eliem Nicole was the fishing village of Kidege's sole lawyer. Quiet and thoughtful, it was a rare problem of any size in the town that didn't eventually find its resolution on Eliem Nicole's desk.

More often than not, the problem's resolution cost the bearer nothing. And everyone knew that Eliem was no altruist; he did it for the sake of the problem. And he had taught her his fascination with problems—with the abstract problem of problems.

Long before he was appointed to the Baina Ya bench, the people of Kidege addressed Eliem Nicole as "Judge." And Tora Soam was Judge Nicole with a strange voice; a voice that was becoming less strange as the seconds passed.

The high-ranking Dracs that had been on the other side of

the table sat in her mind as any greying, overweight collection of human officials would. Zigh Caida, the First Deputy of the Chamber, even had a face fixed in her mind. She thought for a long time, and then remembered: it was the Vice-commander of Storm Mountain, General Dell's, face. Kindly, old General Dell.

Morio used to say that the General had adopted himself as my father. In a way, it had been true.

She shook her head and moved to the edge of the sleeping platform. She felt as though she were in the center of an enormous puzzle; a game with no rules, no objectives, no purpose. Lita teasing its students with its "I win" game; caught in the web of an unknown logos. And her mind felt the need of a purpose; a need to know the rules.

"Well, Nicole, you know at least one thing: these creatures are Dracs, not humans." The knotting in her gut as she made that statement told her more: they were not friends; they were deadly enemies.

If I could just see! Damn it, if I could just see!

She touched the edge of that well of self-pity; and backed away from it. And, from the pages of the Talman, Namvaac spoke to her.

And the student said to Namvaac, "Jetah, the darkness covers all the Universe. It is such an all-powerful evil, I feel so small and helpless within it. Next to this darkness, the black of death seems so bright."

Namvaac studied the hooked blade, then handed it back to the student. "Where you are now, child, Tochalla has been before you. It, too, was in darkness. It, too, had a knife. But Tochalla also had talma."

She sat straight up and strained her ears as a slight difference in sound touched the air. She turned her head right, then left, trying fruitlessly to determine the direction from which the sound was coming. Because of the curved, sound-absorbing walls of the sleeping room, the sound appeared to come from all directions.

Nicole pushed herself up, felt her way to the sleeping room door, and opened it. The sounds became slightly louder— something between glass air chimes and a guitar.

Music. The notes appeared to follow no familiar pattern. It was an incomprehensible wandering through minor scales. Sad, lonely wandering.

She pressed the control that opened all of the doors, then felt her way to the apartment entrance. The sounds came from her left. She hesitated. She had never been down that part of the corridor.

Nicole placed her left hand against the stones of the corridor wall and began feeling her way toward the sounds. As she walked along, several times the playing stopped, then resumed with a different but equally incomprehensible tune. She followed the sounds until the acoustic response to the instrument told her that she was across the corridor from a large, high-ceilinged chamber. She entered the room, leaned against the wall, and listened.

The music took on a mournful, haunting quality; and she let herself open to it devoid of comparisons or preconceptions. Then the music spoke to her, calling up familiar but strangely combined emotions. The music stopped, but Nicole let the memory of the dying notes stroke her thoughts.

"Who is that? Speak?" The voice was Tora Kia's.

"Can you not see me, Tora Kia?"

"No. The chamber is dark. What do you want?"

"I heard you playing. I thought you could no longer play . . . because of your arm."

"I can still play with the other."

There was movement, then steps coming toward her. She tensed, but Kia only took her by her arm and led her toward a couch. Nicole sat down and listened as the Drac moved away and again took up its instrument and played an odd assortment of notes. The playing stopped. "In your apartment, Joanne Nicole, I heard you cry out."

"It was nothing but a dream."

"Baadek told me that you did not speak to my parent about what happened in the car. I should thank you."

"I kept silent more for Baadek's sake than for yours, Kia."

A quiet laugh. "Of course. Still, I apologize for my actions and thank you for yours."

She remained silent and Kia again began playing its instrument. The sounds were alien, but the instrument was the tidna: a harp with strings made of glass. But the music was different for another, indefinable reason. She let her head fall back upon the couch and listened, allowing the peculiar musical phrases to occupy her awareness. The music changed slightly, and the patterns became something she could identify—feel familiar with.

"Kia, what is that?"

The music stopped. "A composition of my own. I wrote it upon Amadeen. Does it speak to you?"

"It incorporates human music; human themes. I recognize them."

"Joanne Nicole, a composition birthed in the blood covering Amadeen would be false unless it carried the sentiments of the Front as well as the Mavedah. Your composer, Tchaikovsky, did much the same for his composition on war. He used the themes of both his nation and that of the enemy."

"What . . . what do you know of human music?"

There was a silence, then she heard the tidna being placed none too gently upon the stone floor. "That human, Mitzak, spoke to me something that seems to be truth. After my parent's game, Mitzak asked me what the difference is between ignorance and stupidity. Mitzak answered his own question by telling me that ignorance is self-inflicted stupidity. I had the feeling that Mitzak was talking about all of us. Both humans and Dracs."

"Your parent's game? Kia, you knew it to be a game? Your performance was a part you played?"

"Of course."

"Why? Why did you cooperate?"

"We live by talma—games. That, and Tora Soam is my parent. It needed my hate for the game."

"But you knew it to be a game."

"It is *all* games, Joanne Nicole. Everything that exists. Did you not absorb anything from listening to *The Talma* when you were in the Chirn Kovah?" Nicole heard the tidna being picked up, then came a series of rapid scales, and combinations of scales. As abruptly as the playing began, it stopped. "I know of Tchaikovsky for the same reason that my parent knows of human behavior and the behaviors of other races. All have been studied in detail. My study was music. My parent studied life. Humans studied us before the war; did they not?"

"Yes."

"Our means of information processing, because of the out-growths of talma, are considerably superior to yours." The strange song birthed in Kia's experience upon Amadeen filled the room. "My parent commands all that can be known about humans; what the humans know, and more."

"The USEF Intelligence Corps—"

"A joke. You see parts of surfaces. We see depths and beyond depths."

"But still you cannot avoid war."

"We cannot avoid it, Joanne Nicole: *we* cannot avoid it." She listened as Kia's Amadeen song continued, the notes becoming almost visible in her mind. And there were gaps; places where notes should have been—would have been except for the musician's missing arm. "And that is how I shall leave it." The tidna was replaced on the floor. "Could you hear where the missing hand should have played?"

"Yes."

"The composition would be untrue to Amadeen if all of the notes were there. This song is crippled, as it must be."

Kia played for a moment, then paused. "It is strange, Joanne Nicole. In the dark like this, you are not . . . not a human. With the darkness of your eyes, do you see the same?"

"Yes. I see us as . . . beings?"

"I heard you cry out. I came to investigate."

"It was only a dream, Tora Kia. I am all right."

It was silent, then Nicole heard Kia stand and move toward her. "I too have dreams, Joanne Nicole." Tora Kia struggled with its thoughts and words. "I need . . . there are things . . . things I wish to talk about."

"Talk to your parent."

Tora Kia hissed a strangled laugh and she heard its boots moving toward the door. "Make your rest, Joanne Nicole."

"Wait." She sat up. "Why me? Why do you want to talk to me?"

The Drac spoke its words as though it were admitting to the greatest sin. "I cannot speak to them—not about war. Not about *my* war. My parent is always the gentle scholar. Baadek has never seen battle. You are a soldier."

"I am a human."

"You are a human *soldier*." The boots moved in front of her, then she felt Tora Kia seat itself on the couch to her left. "Do you not see that I have more in common with you than I have with my own race?"

The silence hung heavily in the room. "I will listen."

"It is perverse that you are the one I come to talk to. But this war is perverse." The sharp smell of happy paste assaulted her nostrils.

Tora Kia remained silent so long that she thought it might have fallen asleep. But then it spoke. "Joanne Nicole, I have moments . . . times when it seems that I am back in battle . . . smell, the noise, the screams—it is all so *real!* . . . And then . . . I am back in the security of my parent's home. I fear for my mind."

Tora Kia laughed. "At the Chirn Kovah, the masters say that I cannot give birth because of my mind. That what I believe will not allow conception to take place. Soon I will be too old; the act of conception would kill me. This will end the Tora line." Then a sigh. "The paste loosens the words—and thoughts—as it dulls perception."

Just the fumes from the drug made her slightly giddy. She reached out a hand and placed it upon Kia's arm, then moved it until her fingers felt Kia's hand holding the tiny container of the sharp-smelling drug. Nicole touched a fintertip to it, then brought the fingertip to her tongue. It stung for an instant, then all sensation of the drug was replaced by a relaxed warmness—

—*Flashes of light and metal splinters; blood, bone, and scraps of flesh; a face made out of pink goo; everything covered with mud*—

In the dark, Tora Kia was a voice; a voice in pain; a voice that wanted her to understand; that might understand her. "I still see the war, Kia. Awake . . . and in my dreams." She was dizzy, and she gently leaned her head against Kia's shoulder, the drug making her head swim. "I wish . . . I wish there was something . . . something we—"

The shoulder moved as Kia laughed. "There are times when I believe that Aakva still plays cruelly with its creatures."

. . . *As though he—it—he were off in the distance, Kia began to talk about Amadeen; the horror of it. —but she saw the horror of Storm Mountain, and cried out. An arm went around her shoulders . . . and she buried her face in Mallik's chest as his hand stroked her face. Strange hand; strange face.*

"Joanne. You are safe, now, Joanne."

. . . *She seemed to fall endless distances, then a softness engulfed her face. Boots walking rapidly away. . . .*

* * *

"Joanne Nicole? Joanne Nicole?"

She opened her eyes, sat up upon the couch, then let her eyes close. "Baadek?"

"Yes, it is Baadek. I have with me the human, Mitzak. Why do you sleep here?"

Nicole pressed her fingers against her temples as icepicks began stirring the syrup between her lobes. "What do you two want?"

"I came to bring you to the morning repast. Since I could not find you, I enlisted Mitzak's help. The morning repast, and Tora Soam, still wait upon you."

She lowered her hands to her lap. "I am not very hungry. I would like to return to my apartments."

Mitzak spoke: "Major, the morning repast includes a beverage with much the same properties, if not the flavor, of coffee."

"You're pretty smug today." Receiving no reply, she stood up and allowed the pair to bring her, first, to her apartments, and then to the dining hall. There she, Mitzak, and Zigh Caida were introduced to the host, Tora Soam. After she had been seated and had sipped from the bowl of hot liquid that had been placed in her hands, Tora Soam's voice came from across the table.

"Joanne Nicole, what is the attraction of this medication Kia uses?"

The throbbing in her head diminishing only slightly, she answered: "I'm sure I don't know."

"As I have, in the past, smelled the substance upon my child, I can now smell it upon you."

"I am not a habitual user, Tora Soam. Its use for me was to cause relaxation, to lower inhibition."

"For what purpose?" She ignored the question and returned her attention to the hot liquid in her bowl. "For what purpose, Joanne Nicole?" The direction of Tora Soam's voice changed. "Mitzak, explain."

"There are different purposes. I cannot read her mind."

An edge crept into the Drac's voice. "The crust beneath your feet is crumbling, human."

"Nevertheless, I cannot read her mind. Nor can I read Kia's mind. You must find your answers from those who can supply them."

"Do you presume to recite *The Talman* to a Drac—to *me?*"

There was a pause, then Tora Soam again spoke: "Mitzak, have you ever used this substance?"

"Yes. But I am only able to tell you my purpose; no one else's."

"And that purpose is?"

"I am able to tell you my purpose; I am not willing. It is none of your concern."

There was a long silence, then Tora Soam spoke quietly. "We are all feeling the pressures of the day's circumstances." The remainder of the repast was conducted in silence.

Later, her headache having subsided, Joanne Nicole warmed in the sunlight as her sandaled feet felt the ancient stone paths of the Tora Estate. Baadek and Mitzak walked with her, each one holding one of her arms above the elbow to guide her. Although one of the hands was human, she could not tell it from the hand of the Drac.

Baadek spoke: "Mitzak, your game with Tora Soam is dangerous."

"It is no more dangerous than yours, Baadek."

"I think you know that there is a difference."

Mitzak snorted out a bitter laugh. "A difference of form, Baadek; not a difference of substance. Tora Soam is not . . . itself these days."

"Are you *insane*, human?"

Joanne Nicole stopped, and pulled her companions to a halt. "If you two are planning on continuing this cryptic conversation, either let me in on it or leave me alone."

Baadek answered. "We cannot leave you here. You could not find your way back." A pause. "We can talk of other things."

"Very well." Nicole stepped off again. "How is Tora Kia?"

"Emmmm. This reminds me. I must leave you with Mitzak." Baadek's footsteps moved quickly down the path ahead of them.

"Mitzak, what is going on?"

"It is complicated."

"I'm a quick study. Explain."

Mitzak sighed and walked in silence. After several minutes he began speaking. "Your meeting with Kia last night; it caused a certain amount of embarrassment."

"What do you mean? The happy paste?"

"No." A pause. "Nicole, what ever did you have in mind to get sexual with Tora Kia?"

She felt the red rushing to her face as she abruptly came to a halt. "I did not! Damn, Mitzak! Kia's a hermaphrodite!"

"Nevertheless."

She pulled her arm from Mitzak's grasp. "Damn you!"

"When you asked me, Nicole, did you want an answer or did you want an opportunity to put on a demonstration?"

"Mitzak, why don't you go and do whatever it is that you do?"

"Do you want me to help you back to your apartments?"

"I can find my own way." Mitzak hesitated for a moment, then his rapid footsteps receded into the silence beyond. Joanne Nicole stood alone, thinking, the sunlight and gentle wind touching her skin. Sexual.

"Absurd. Besides being hermaphrodites, the parts are in the wrong places."

She turned her face away from the sunlight and felt with her feet for the edge of the path. How could a human, male or female, be sexual with a Drac? In training, the brief survey of Drac reproduction was enough to evaporate any pervert's fantasies regarding human-Drac fun and games. Male and female organs were contained in the lower abdomen behind the lips of a belly-slit.

In the ancient True Laws of Aakva, Rhada had said that it is law that at least one child out of three be made by joining one's fluids with the fluids of another. The lips could extend, joining a pair and allowing fertilization to occur by another. But it was not something a human could participate in without considerable surgery.

Still, she thought. Last night . . . *she cried out. An arm went around her shoulders . . . and she buried her face in Mallik's chest as his hand stroked her face. Strange hand; strange face.*

"Joanne. You are safe, now, Joanne . . . ."

As she edged her way back to her apartments, she could not shake the memory.

13

There will come to you at times a blinding vision that fills your eyes and mind, announcing itself as Truth. Step back and strike down this vision and beat it as though it were a brain-sucking monster.

Then, with it lying there limp, bent, and tarnished, if it still claims to be Truth, accept it with great caution, remembering that the most dangerous lies arrive in the most highly polished armor.

—Aydan and The War of Ages, Koda Itheda,
The Talman

After the night repast, she sat on a cushion in the music room, the tidna balanced on her lap. With untrained fingers she roughly plucked from the glass strings a version of Kia's Amadeen tune. There were familiar footsteps, and she continued playing as she spoke. "Where have you been today, Kia?"

The footsteps paused, then there was the sound of the Drac lowering itself into the softness of the couch facing her. "Your playing is pitiful, human."

She stopped playing and placed the tidna on the floor. "Kia, last night—"

"I do not wish to discuss it."

She smiled. "Then why are you here?"

"The playing . . . I came to protect my instrument." There was a long silence, then came a chuckle from the Drac. "Joanne Nicole, what did last night mean to you?"

She let her hands fall to her lap. "I'm not sure. For a moment I imagined you as my husband—former husband; he's dead. I reached out for . . . I don't know. Comfort. Security. Peace."

"And you found these things?"

She slowly nodded her head. "Yes. Yes, I did. What was last night to you?"

The sharp smell of Kia's drug filled the room. "Would you care for some?"

"No. What was last night to you?"

"Perhaps it was the same for me."

"I don't believe that, Kia. Everyone on the Tora estate seems very upset about it. I don't understand why. Did you tell them about last night?"

"There was no need to. Joanne Nicole, we are both trapped in the limits of a carefully engineered talma. What happened last night was not expected. It fell outside the limits and was, therefore, quite obvious to those familiar with the talma."

"Will you tell me?"

"I . . . I cannot." Kia stood and left the room.

She leaned back on her elbows and sat in the quiet loneliness for an hour or more, when a slight difference in the air caused her to stand and listen.

The air seemed to move slightly, there was a vibration she could feel through her feet, and she could hear the gentle rattle of glass. Shock waves coming from a great distance. Nicole felt her way around the furniture until she came to an outside wall. She placed her hands against the stones and moved along the wall until she came to a window.

The vibrations became more pronounced; then there came the familiar crump of sonic warheads.

"Damn! Oh, damn!"

The USEF was attacking Draco.

She staggered away from the window and ran for the corridor, smacking into sharp edges, stumbling to the floor. After making it into the corridor, she turned left and let the fingers of her right hand glide along the wall as she ran toward her apartment. Once in the doorway, she immediately closed the door to the corridor, went through the central access into the sleeping room, and closed that door too.

As the sounds of the attack grew louder, she buried her face in the cushions and covers, much like a child trying to hide from the dark. But her dark was something that couldn't be hidden from. Then, as abruptly as they had begun, the sounds ceased. She sat up, facing the door, clutching one of the cushions, waiting for them to come for her.

There was—not a dream—a kaleidoscope of impressions; shards of some indefinable whole. . . .

. . . They were discussing the game much as, in the past, she had seen humans chewing over a bridge or poker hand. . . .

. . . *In the Chirn Kovah I had been placed in what amounted to a sensory deprivation environment. . . .*

No sight; no touch; reduced sound . . . and then *The Talman* handed to her for entertainment.

. . . The strangeness—the alien unknown—of everything was made almost familiar because the images from her eyes were prevented from overpowering her other senses. . . .

. . . *A strange thought is in my mind: I was curious; but, if I could have seen, I would have been terrified. . . .*

"*. . . To Tora Soam, the war is . . . an immense puzzle to be solved; a fascinating problem. I think my parent basks in the size and complexity of the puzzle. You and I are nothing more than two factors among the trillions that comprise this puzzle. . . .*"

. . . They had been dipped in fire and had survived to see the Drac Infantry pulling back. Morio Taiseido collapsed beside her, his voice hoarse.

"Major, I could die content at this moment. We whipped them! Holy son of a bitch, we whipped them!"

. . . *Is this joy the appeal to battle; to war? If it was the truth, it would be an impossible motivation to treat rationally.*

The rules were out; the ultimate consequences were out; nothing was in our minds except the fact that the Dracs were falling back. In that minuscule particle of time, we were victorious. . . .

• • •

"...*you have overlooked the two most important parties to the negotiations. Where is the Mavedah? Where is the Amadeen Front?*"

Raga Gia snorted out a scornful laugh.

"I refuse, Tora Kia, to have the Front at the talks."

Its voice changed direction. "Does this comply with your game, Soam?"

Game?

Raga's voice turned again in Kia's direction. "The humans will represent the interests of the Front, and the Dracs will represent the interests of the Mavedah."

Tora Kia laughed. "No, no, my parent's most respected guest. The interests of the Dracon Chamber are not identical to those of the Mavedah."

Sergeant Benbo spoke for the first time. "Raga Gia, if the Front is not part of the negotiations, there can be no peace. If negotiations ever happen, the Amadeen Front will want its own representative. The Front only wants an end to the war under certain terms. It is the same with the Mavedah."

...Zigh grumped. "Very well, each side should formulate its goals—what it hopes to achieve from the negotiations. Once we have all seen the diagrams—"

Nicole spoke: "There will be no diagrams, First Deputy. Human negotiators are not familiar with talma."

"Surely there must be a human equivalent?"

"Situation assessment, goal formulation, and path construction and evaluation are not systemized comprehensive disciplines among human negotiators."

Exasperated wheezing seemed to come from First Deputy Zigh's direction. The wheezing paused.

"Goals must be stated in *some* manner!"

Mitzak laughed....

"...*the facilities at the Talman Kovah have projected an armed truce with the forces of the United States of Earth.*"

"There are several things upon which the occurrence and successful exploitation of this projected truce depend. The truce will follow immediately after a battle of certain configurations...."

"...*if there is to be peace, or if there is to be more war, sense dictates that talma is best followed if the result is a matter of studied choice rather than a matter of ignorance, anger, or accident. One does not need to take to diagrams to see the truth in that...."*

...And then, as though it were being played before her upon a stage, she remembered The Story of Lita in the Koda Ovsinda.

Lita had invented a game for the students to play....

...There was disturbed silence from the Drac side of the table until Ovjetah Suinat Piva of the Fangen Kovah burst out in laughter.

"I see your game, Tora Soam. Very clever, and you have my compliments."

Compliments?
A game?
A goddamned game....

Her breath coming in rapid gasps, she awakened on her side, still clutching the cushion. There was quiet around her. The sounds of attack had ended.

She released the cushion and pushed herself to a sitting position. The pieces of her dream blurred and faded. Her stomach told her that it was past time for the morning repast.

Why hasn't Baadek come?

She stood up, felt her way to the door, and opened it along with the door to the greeting room. Her ears told her that the door to the corridor was closed, which answered the question to why Baadek hadn't called. The closed outside door was the Drac equivalent of a do not disturb sign.

She opened the door, but could hear no one in the corridor. Closing the central door to the greeting room, she spent a few moments cleaning up and putting on a fresh robe. When she was finished, she left her apartment and began feeling her way down the corridor to her right. As she approached the entrance to the series of large living and entertainment chambers, she heard voices.

One of the voices belonged to Tora Kia. Nicole did not enter the chamber, but stood out of sight in the corridor, listening.

"When will you take command of your new denve, Kia?" The voice was unfamiliar to her.

"It depends. I am on a special mission for our parent at the present. How long the mission will take is conjecture. What of you? How long is it before you have to report to the Denve Itheda?"

"Only a few days. The wound is nothing."

"A third officer. You must be the youngest one in the Denvedah. I am proud of you. Our parent is proud, too, Vidak."

Vidak.

Sin Vidak.

The child I supposedly saved from the fire.

A third officer?

But this one's voice was different—too different—too old.

"There were a great many promotions after the battle of Fyrine IV, Kia." Nicole heard one of them stand and begin walking about the chamber. There was a silence, more walking, then a pause. "What is this? Kia, by my narrow ass, it is a *human!*"

Nicole heard Kia stand, walk into the corridor, and approach her. "Why, Vidak, don't you remember? This is the woman who saved you from the fire at Ditaar."

There was an overly long pause. Then the one called Vidak spoke: "Of course . . . and how does the morning find you . . ."

"Joanne Nicole," Kia completed.

"Yes, how does the morning find you, Joanne Nicole?"

Nicole leaned heavily against the wall as the edges of truth and lie swept across her darkness. There was an instant when tears and anger fought with a million blasphemies; but she remembered the student from the Aakva Kovah.

And Shizumaat told Namndas that both the truth and the lie must be tested.

"Test the truth by forcing it to lie; test the lie by forcing it to be true."

She reached out a hand. "You are Sin Vidak?"

"Yes." There was a moment of tenseness, then she felt the warm fingers of the Drac's hands enclose hers.

"It is good to see you again, Joanne Nicole."

Nicole moistened her dry lips. "Perhaps you can tell me something I've always wanted to know?"

"If I can."

"What happened to your three classmates that I dragged from the fire along with yourself?"

"Ehhhh . . ." The Drac's fingers tensed. "They are all well."

Nicole nodded. "All three of them?"

"Yes."

She released the Drac's hand. "There were only two others."

Tora Kia interrupted. "Vidak was very young and afraid at the time, Joanne Nicole. Who can remember such things under such circumstances?"

A million talman paths raced across her mind, intersecting, finding blocks, reaching conclusions. "Vidak, I overheard Kia say that you are a third officer."

There was a moment of uncomfortable movement, then Sin Vidak spoke. "Eh . . . perhaps we should talk more at a later time, Joanne Nicole. You do not look well."

"When I was in the Chirn Kovah, I was told that you had entered the Tsien Denvedah."

"I am Tsien Denvedah."

"How much time did your initial training take?"

"Ehh . . . this is not—"

"Vidak," Kia interrupted, "perhaps you should inform our parent that Joanne Nicole—"

"How much *time*, Vidak?" Both of them became very quiet. Nicole reached out her right hand and wrapped her fingers around Vidak's wrist. "I'll tell you how long, Sin Vidak; it used to be my job to know. Tsien Denvedah initial training lasts a quarter of a year. Your advanced infantry training took half a year. And you are a third officer. The Tsien Denvedah doesn't jump ranks in promotions, and in no case is there allowed less than half a year between grades. How long is that, Drac?"

". . . Please—"

"How *long?*" She released Vidak's arm. "Does six years sound about right? Six years, minimum?"

Tora Kia made a clucking sound, and Nicole heard Sin Vidak walk down the corridor. "Joanne Nicole, you were badly injured—"

"Six years, Kia? *Six years!* Are you going to try and make me believe that it has been six years since I regained consciousness? Time flies when you're having fun?"

"I do not understand—"

"I want some answers. And I want them *now*."

Tora Kia shouted. "Gedji! Gedji!"

Nicole heard footsteps running in the distance. The sound stopped. "Yes, Tora Kia?"

"Ask my parent to come to the green chamber."

"Tora Soam is meeting with First Deputy Zigh."

Kia chuckled. "Tell my parent that Joanne Nicole and Sin Vidak have met, and that Vidak is a little older than the human remembers."

"*Ai!* . . . at once, Tora Kia." The footsteps of the one called Gedji hit top speed and moved from the corridor.

Kia took Nicole's arm and led her into the chamber. "Do not blame Vidak for any of this. It was not part of the game." She was led to a couch and she sat down. Nicole heard Kia take its place upon another couch. "You are angry, Joanne Nicole; but it will pass."

"I spent my tears on a child called Sin Vidak."

"I know."

Again her mind sought paths as another piece of puzzle presented itself. Nicole leaned back in the couch. "Kia, it is unfortunate that Dracs are hermaphrodites."

"Why?"

"There are some names that I would like to call you that you cannot properly appreciate with your current arrangement of organs."

"Emmmm."

There were hushed voices and rapid footsteps in the corridor outside the chamber. Then Tora Soam and Zigh Caida shouting in relays at Sin Vidak. Kia issued a sad chuckle. "Poor Vidak. This is a sorry homecoming for a hero of the Tsien Denvedah."

14

The unintentional chain of events we call an accident describes paths as real as any path planned, diagrammed, and executed in principle with talma. And if the accident alters the present to the more desirable future, this special kind of path has the advantage of having already been proven valid.

—The Story of Lita, Koda Ovsinda, *The Talman*

The green chamber was silent for a long time. It was so quiet Nicole could almost hear Tora Soam's eyeballs click as they moved from Tora Kia, to her, to Zigh Caida, and then back to Kia. Tora Soam eventually broke the silence. "Joanne Nicole, what do you know?"

"As someone once told me, that is a question that would take many hours to answer. It would be more efficient if you told me what I *should* know."

There was a silence, then a sigh. "This is a disaster." Tora Soam's voice changed direction. "Zigh Caida, I am at a loss as to what to tell you."

"Soam, do I detect panic in your manner? This is not disaster, but accident." Zigh actually sounded unconcerned.

Kia laughed. "My parent, is this how the Ovjetah of the Talman Kovah approaches its problems? Was last night's attack instructive? Has the war suddenly become more to you than an amuzing puzzle?" Such disrespect, such sarcasm, even from Kia, was abnormal.

Tora Soam answered, its words dripping acid. "Kia, your mouth follows unproductive paths."

"My many, many apologies, my parent. And, now, to Joanne Nicole's request?"

"Why did no one tell me Vidak was coming home?"

"Vidak wanted to surprise us." Again Kia laughed.

"Your amusement is out of place, Kia."

Nicole leaned forward on the couch, her elbows resting upon her knees. "I want some answers. Your family squabbles can wait. Tora Soam? Was there an attack last night; or was that a special effects demonstration put on for my benefit?"

"That attack was . . . real. Too real."

"Talk to her, my parent. Talk to her."

"Yes . . . it is a time for answers. You are correct, Zigh Caida, it is an accident. If the paths its events describe are valid has yet to be proven, however."

Nicole heard one of the Dracs stand. Then Zigh Caida spoke. "Kia, I think Soam would rather perform this task alone with the human."

"But, First Deputy, I really do want to watch."

Tora Soam spoke: "I agree with the First Deputy, Kia. Joanne Nicole's need for answers outweighs your desire to see . . . your parent squirm. In answer to your question, Kia; this puzzle never was amusing, as I am certain someone important to you will eventually point out."

There was a brief silence, and then she heard Kia stand. Both Kia and the First Deputy walked from the chamber. Nicole leaned back in the couch. "Well?"

"It is long in the telling, Joanne Nicole."

"Time is all I have."

"It is difficult to know where to begin. Do you have any specific questions?"

"I can think of one: how many of you motherless kizlodes participated in this charade?"

"Emmmm. I do not have an exact number. Hundreds. You are not the only human involved. Chance just happened to favor you."

"Chance?"

"Your blindness."

"My—is my blindness part of this charade? *Am* I blind?"

". . . Yes. You have no reason to believe me; but it is the truth."

"Have I been . . . did you people *blind* me?"

"No. No." There were sounds of movement; then footsteps crossing the floor to her right. "Joanne Nicole, explain to me the basic purpose and structure of talma."

"Kiss my sitting-end, Drac! I am not one of your students. I—"

"Joanne Nicole, you will do as I say! Otherwise, I cannot meet your request. The work of years is at stake. Now tell me the basic purpose and structure of talma."

Nicole spent a few seconds nibbling on the skin of her lower lip. "Very well. The purpose is the achievement of goals. The general structure is to know the present, to know the alterations of the present needed to make the achievement of the goal a future reality, and to discover, assess, and choose the paths that lead from the present to the desired future."

"Adequate."

"I had nothing else with which to occupy my time in the Chirn Kovah. It is no great accomplishment."

Tora Soam snorted out a laugh. "There have been students who have learned less with eyes and more time."

"So what is the point?"

"That *is* the point."

The footsteps moved from her right to her left. "Joanne Nicole, let me tell you something about the war that you do not know. Although it is comprised of a vast multiplicity of presents and goals, the war is still an event that should fit within the basic structure of talma. We are in a present; there is a more desirable future; all that is left is to discover and execute the paths from the first to the second."

"And?"

More footsteps, then a pause. "We appear to be out of paths. Do you recall and understand the object lesson of the night repast? The discussion between Tora Kia and Amos Benbo?"

"The object lesson was simple enough, Tora Soam. All parties involved cannot have everything that they want. The goals of the Mavedah and those of the Front are mutually exclusive."

"Emmmm. Tell me the difference between an apparent and a real goal."

"The apparent goal is the one perceived and stated; the real goal is the one that will satisfy the difference between the present and the desired future."

Nicole felt Tora Soam lower itself beside her upon the couch. "What are the apparent and the real goals of the Mavedah and the Front?"

The apparent goals were clear: each side demanded nothing less than the extermination of the other side. The real goals? The settling of old scores? Happiness? Put the entire planet's population under therapy until each side can live with the existence of the other? "I am not certain."

"Emmmm. I will tell you this: as things now stand, both the Dracon Chamber and the United States of Earth would be inclined to hand back conquered territories and end the fighting—except for Amadeen."

"Have there already been negotiations?"

Tora Soam hissed. "Of a sort. A creature more of information and communication, rather than accomplishment." The silence in the chamber became desperate.

The Drac seemed to be waiting for Nicole to respond. She rubbed her temples and thought for a moment. "Zigh Caida and the other Dracs at the repast; they are the Drac representatives to the negotiations?"

"The . . . former negotiations."

. . . And then the past spoke to her:

Uhe told its warmasters:

"Never again shall one tribe starve because of a boundary, tabu, or law. . . ."

The student Shizumaat spoke to the servant of Aakva:

". . . I see that a rule stood between the Mavedah and survival; I see that the rule was nothing sacred, but made by Sindie; and I see that Uhe saw this and cast the rule aside to save its people. The truth I see, then, is that rules are meant to serve the Sindie; the Sindie is not meant to serve rules. . . ."

In some manner, every crisis described in *The Talman* was rooted in *talmai veruhune:* the service of rules; ruleboundedness. Every resolution was rooted in stepping outside of the rules. And talma was the formal discipline, paths, rules for stepping outside of rules.

Maltak Di, in the Koda Nushada, told its students: "Talma

is not *the* way; Talma is *a* way for seeking ways."

Ruleboundedness. And every major halt in human advancement, every major crisis in human history, was rooted in *talmai veruhune*. Call it religion, politics, philosophy, science—it was the blind allegiance to rules.

"Tora Soam, both the United States of Earth and the Dracon Chamber are rulebound into this war."

"Yes."

"And you find through me a way to step outside of the rules?"

"A possible way."

Too many things came together at once as sharp pains lanced through her head. She could not—would not—admit to what she knew; what Tora Soam wanted her to know; and what the Ovjetah would have her do about it.

...There was a disturbed silence from the Drac side of the table until Ovjetah Suinat Piva of the Fangen Kovah burst out in laughter.

"I see your game, Tora Soam...."

Nicole stood up. "I must go to my apartments, Tora Soam. I do not feel well. I think I, too, see your game."

She heard Tora Soam stand. "And what will you do?" Nicole began feeling her way toward the corridor. "What will you do, Joanne Nicole?"

Nicole sat in her apartment's entertainment room for a few minutes, trying to get control of herself. Then she said to hell with it and began tearing up the place. Nicole ripped open the cushions with her fingers and swung things until she heard other things smash.

"Cute! *Cute,* Tora Soam, you bastard—"

Lights flashed in her head and she found herself sitting on the floor, a lump growing on the right side of her forehead. Cut stone walls do not smash easily.

"This is stupid."

She pulled herself up, felt her way into the bathing room, and tried to keep the swelling down by putting cold water on her forehead.

The game.

Lita's formula for winning: *"I win."*

The bloody damned game.

She realized that she had been fenced with rules and fattened up with choice tidbits of information. Tora Soam and the other Jetai Talman had found themselves rulebound. Somehow a Lita had fenced Amadeen, the USEF, and the Dracon Chamber with a structure of rules...a structure that allowed no end to the war...no end short of destroying both human and Drac civilizations. The weapons were too powerful; the tacticians too skilled.

An insight was needed: a talma that would reveal the nature of the structure, which would, in turn, reveal the talma that would allow the structure to be encircled by another structure.

And she was a part of the talma to find that insight. Paths for finding paths to find paths through which more paths...

Wheels within bloody wheels.

She stood upright. —*That's why I could never get that damned feeler stick in the Chirn Kovah to work for me! That would have allowed me to see too much! Another damned talma to find....*

Pur Sonaan and its damned player...selected recitals by Vencha Eban...

...Vencha Eban gasping at being discovered not cleaning the room... *"After the birth of my only child, Hiurod, my reproductive organs (poignant pause indicating deep sorrow) had to be removed. Hiurod died—"*

"God *damn*it!"

Supporting cast: Vunseleh, Mitzak...*Tegara—oh, she was good.*

"Your name—ha! Your skin! It is yellow!
"No shit, toadface...."
...*Tora Kia slapping me in anger...good old Baadek swearing its undying loyalty to me....*

They were all good.

"Jesus H. Christ!"

And if everything fit together, Tora Soam would be standing in her open doorway, watching its convoluted talma going down the drain. Nicole turned toward the bathing room door, felt her way through the central accessway, and entered the greeting room.

"Tora Soam?"

"Yes?"

"You bastards certainly went to a lot of trouble. Why?"

"To end a war is not sufficient reason?"

"Why *me?*"

"You were one of many, Dracs and humans with unique sights, selected by the Talman Kovah's computers. Your command's unpredictable resistance at Storm Mountain placed you in the coarse selection. Your rescue of the children—"

"Was . . . was *that* attack staged, too?"

"No. But I suppose it is to be expected that you would put nothing beyond my behavior."

"That is no lie, Tora Soam."

Nicole held her hands to her head. *Benbo and that smell of flowers . . . cleaning, Vencha Eban!*

"Damn! Is Benbo? A Drac?"

Tora Soam gave an involuntary laugh. "My apologies. Your Amos Benbo is still on Ditaar."

"Who . . ."

"Its name is Fanda, one of our most accomplished actors."

"A Drac?"

"Yes. It was necessary for you to hear the Amadeen Front's hate from someone you could trust. Fanda studied Benbo for many days." Tora Soam was silent for a moment. "It will harm things no further, Joanne Nicole, for me to inform you of something else. It may relieve some of your pain. Leonid Mitzak, under my instructions, lied to you about the extent of the attack on the V'Butaan Field. None of your men were killed."

Nicole leaned against the wall. A thousand thoughts demanded her attention at the same time.

. . . On my way to Draco, drugged and dreaming, my memories of Mallik and my unborn child . . . Morio, Benbo, and scenes of the battle of Storm Mountain. . . .

. . . At the university, I never told anyone about Mallik or the child I gave up—

. . . The humming . . . that humming!

"Those dreams I had. They . . . they were about things that never took place!"

"This is partly true—"

"Damnit! What haven't you messed with?"

"You are blind, Joanne Nicole; and there is still a war, and a problem to be solved."

She heard Tora Soam's footsteps approach her, then a hand took her arm.

"Come with me. You have rendered your apartment unfit

for habitation. I will have it cleaned and the furnishings replaced." They entered the corridor and turned to the right.

"Joanne Nicole, to follow this talma it was necessary to enable you to see both as a human and as a Drac. Perhaps Sin Vidak's unfortunate timing has destroyed this. Perhaps not. As long as it works, an accidental trigger to your thoughts serves as well as one that is planned. But all of the sides to this war are rulebound."

"That much I saw."

"Excellent. Can you see whether we are bound by our own rules, or by the rules of an outside agent?"

Nicole shook her head. "No. But the answer is on Amadeen. Of course, you knew that."

"Yes. We knew the answer is there. We also knew that we did not know what questions to ask to get that answer. Our negotiators are attempting to open again the talks with the humans. Will you go with us to Amadeen?"

"Answer me this, first: Vencha Eban at the Chirn Kovah..."

"Fanda also played that part."

Images, vocal gestures, came together in her mind. The disrespectful words; the hesitations before saying the word "parent."

"Tora Soam is not...itself these days."

"Fanda is an excellent actor, Tora Soam."

"I will pass along your compliment."

Nicole stopped and faced the Drac. "When does all of this testing end?"

"I do not understand."

"You are another actor. And this is yet another play. When does this testing end?"

The Drac was silent for a moment, then answered in a different, higher voice. "I think it already has."

15

"'Choice' is not an empty word that I use, Arlan; it is the nature of our race. To be alive is to have the ability to have goals; to be of this special life, is to have the ability to choose; and to choose anything is to choose goals. . . .

"Without a goal you are simply taking up space— not only in this room, and this kovah, but in this Universe.

"Either find a goal, or turn the space over to one who does have a goal."
—The Story of Maltak Di, Koda Nuschada, *The Talman*

Joanne Nicole sat in the back of a car, Baadck driving her to what it said was the Talman Kovah—

What I assume to be the back of a car; what I assume to be driving; by a creature I assume to be Baadek

"Driver, who are you?"

"You do not recognize me, Joanne Nicole? I am Baadek."

"Who *are* you?"

The Drac chuckled. "My name is Hida Mu."

"Another actor?"

145

"I belong to the same company as Fanda."

Nicole rubbed her eyes, the motion of the car moving her— *What I assume to be a car; what I assume to be driving*— There were Shizumaat's words, and she remembered them: *"Instead believe this: question everything, accept the wholeness of no truth nor the absolute rightness of any path."*

Her hand reached out and felt for the doorlatch. When she found the recessed handle, she pushed on it, the door opened, and she began to step out of the compartment.

A curse came from the driver's seat, the sound of hissing brakes, as Nicole's right foot was whipped out from under her, flinging her against the open door. A strong hand grabbed her left arm as the vehicle slewed to a stop.

The driver relaxed its grip on her, and Nicole relaxed her grip on the door, sinking down upon the road's pavement. "You are insane! Poorzhab!" A door opened and Nicole could hear boots running around the vehicle, then the Drac squatted next to her. "Are you hurt? The Ovjetah will have my feet in a fire for this—oh, look at your knee!"

"I cannot look at much of anything, Drac." She gingerly reached out and touched her right knee. "It's only scraped. Don't have a hemorrhage over it."

"Why? Joanne Nicole, why did you do this to me?"

"It was necessary to test the truth by trying to make it lie. Isn't that what you kizlodes have been teaching me? Trust nothing?"

"Ahhh! You do not test the sharpness of a knife by plunging the blade into your skull, do you?" Hands reached under her armpits and lifted her back into the car. After her legs had been lifted in and her door slammed shut, Nicole half-heard a string of muttered curses as the Drac driver moved around the vehicle and slammed its own door. Nicole presumed that the subsequent rapid clicks of metal against metal were the doors being locked. "Now, I beg you, just sit until we arrive at the kovah!"

The vehicle jerked into motion. "Drac?"

After a steaming silence, the Drac answered. "What?"

"How do I test that it *is* the Talman Kovah, Drac?"

"That . . . *that* is *not* my problem, human! *Not* my problem!"

Nicole rested her head against the back of the seat as the evidence from her most recent experiment throbbed in her knee.

* * *

Trust in mere words was in thin supply.

She was left, seated in a couch. After the Drac driver had left, Nicole stood up and felt her way around the room. It was a relatively small greeting room; two couches, two doors on opposite ends, the walls and floor covered in smooth tiles. She returned to the couch.

There was the sound of a door opening, then soft, unfamiliar footsteps entering the room. The sounds of the footsteps ceased.

"Welcome, Joanne Nicole, to the Talman Kovah. My name is Ovjetah Tora Soam."

The voice was different—different from the one she had heard in the Chirn Kovah—different from the one she had heard at the Tora estate—*always supposing that I had been at the Tora estate.*

The one calling itself Tora Soam continued: "I see questions upon your face. I am inclined to answer a few. What would you ask?"

"The Tora Soam I know is different."

"Does that surprise you?"

"No. . . . No. I am developing a high surprise threshold."

"Excellent."

"But this game . . . it is grotesque!"

"It is for a purpose. You would not be here unless you understood that purpose." There was a silence; then the sound of the Drac—if it was a Drac—seating itself in the opposite couch.

"Drac, at times, I think I know the purpose; at other times, I don't know."

"Do you have questions?"

Do I have questions? Hell, yes, I have questions! Will I get a straight answer to any of them?

"Drac, the one called Tora Kia."

"Yes?"

"Is Tora Kia—the one *I* met—is that your first child?"

"Yes."

"Were my experiences with Tora Kia genuine?"

The new one called Tora Soam laughed. "A fine word: genuine. Yes. I suppose they were; if anything can be considered genuine. Kia was not happy with my game. Its experiences upon Amadeen clouded Kia's sense of talma. I understand that Mitra Quim played *my* part with true conviction."

"Was Kia's part staged?"

Another laugh. "Partly, but not the part that you mean. I can only speculate about the frustratedness of your, emmmm, love affair."

Nicole felt her face turn red. "How did you know about that meeting?"

"Kia told me. My child is sufficiently versed in talma to know that it might have destroyed my plans with its exercise in self pity. As it turns out, however, no damage was done. Your meeting with Sin Vidak may be another matter, however. We can only see."

"Drac—"

"My proper address is 'Ovjetah,' or 'Tora Soam.'"

"I've been told that before, Drac."

"Emmmm."

"In fact, I have no evidence that you even *are* a Drac. Your Fanda—if that's its name—played a fairly convincing human."

Nicole heard motion from the other couch, then three footsteps. A hand took hers. "Count the fingers, human."

She felt the three-fingered hand with both of hers; then she stood, moving her hands up the Drac's arm, shoulder, and throat, until her fingertips were touching the creature's face. The smooth skin, the almost absent nose, the prominent brow . . . the mouth opened. "Are you satisfied, now?"

Nicole moved her hands down the Drac's chest, then she grabbed its robe with two angry fists. "Your face might be a costume! Perhaps I ought to rip off this robe and check out your piping to be certain!"

Strong hands grabbed her wrists, pulling her hands free from the robe. "Sit down, Joanne Nicole." The hands held her wrists until she lowered herself down upon the couch. The hands released her. There were the sounds of the Drac returning to the other couch. "You are the graduate of a process. You have discovered what the process is intended to serve—which was part of your graduation. You hold a piece of the answer needed to resolve this war." The Drac stood; its footsteps moved across the floor. "In the time that it has taken me to say that, over two hundred Drac and human soldiers have either died or have been wounded." Tora Soam's footsteps moved around for a few moments, then came to a stop. "You had a question."

"What makes me so special in this process? I was told that hundreds were involved."

"Yes." There was a silence. "But two things have happened: your graduation came early—due to the chance circumstance of Vidak's visit; and the United States of Earth and the Dracon Chamber are close to agreeing upon the terms of a cease-fire."

"The cease-fire terms?"

"The terms are similar to those suggested by all of you who were in training, except that the Ninth Quadrant Assembly has requested and has obtained permission to have a committee from the assembly observe the negotiations."

"The Ninth Quadrant?" Nicole frowned as something buzzed in her head. "For what purpose?"

"The stated purpose, Joanne Nicole, is to observe and report back to the Quadrant Assembly."

"Do you suspect another purpose?"

"I suspect everything; don't you?"

Nicole slowly nodded. "Tora Soam, what are the other cease-fire terms?"

"I see I am Tora Soam, now."

"For the time being."

"Emmmm. As to the terms, the human and Drac forces will halt all advancement and will establish fixed positions; a de-militarized zone will be established upon Amadeen; and the zone will be policed by a joint human-Drac force. And, as you know, neither the zone nor its police will be able to halt the fighting upon Amadeen."

Nicole heard the Drac resume its seat upon the opposite couch. "Soon a joint human-Drac commission will be established to supervise the return of captured territories, as well as the colonization of new planets. Of course, as you have pointed out, the cease-fire upon Amadeen cannot turn into a treaty unless a solution is found for Amadeen. But that cannot be done until we discover how we are rulebound."

Nicole settled back upon her couch. "Maybe I'll help you in this. But not if you keep pulling twists on me. I have to have something I can rely upon; some reference points to reality; something to trust."

Then the Drac spoke the words of Shizumaat: "'Instead, believe this: question everything, accept the wholeness of no truth, nor the absolute rightness of any path. Make this your dogma and in it you will find eventual comfort and security; for in this dogma is your right to rule the lower creatures of the Universe; for in this dogma is your right to choose your talma; for in this dogma stands your right to freedom from dogma.'"

"Tora Soam, that last piece of advice almost killed me."

"Joanne Nicole, talma does not assure immortality; it only improves your chances of achieving goals." Tora Soam's voice seemed to turn away. "You are not required to either like it or approve of it, human. But you must understand it. We will be leaving for Amadeen in a few days, and it will take many more days for us to reach the negotiations before the cease-fire fails. Will you come with me to Amadeen?"

"Who else will be going?"

"Some of my advisors from the Talman Kovah. There will also be Leonid Mitzak and my firstborn, Tora Kia."

"Why?"

"Both Mitzak and Kia understand your function in this enterprise. Their task is to help you."

"What function will you serve, Tora Soam?"

"I will advise our negotiators."

"And what function will I serve?"

"You will advise me."

Joanne Nicole wiped her hands across her face, letting them fall upon her lap. "I don't have your answers."

The Drac issued a brief laugh. "Events do not allow me to wait for them. The answers are upon Amadeen. Will you come?"

"Do I have a choice?"

"Of course. I cannot force you to find my answers."

"You people have certainly done a fine task of trying."

"Your sightlessness and I governed the kind and nature of the information you received. We did not force you. You came to your own conclusions through your own choices. Joanne Nicole, will you come to Amadeen with me?"

"I want to tell you 'No!' Because . . . because you have not dealt with me . . ."

"I suggest the word 'fairly' to complete your thought. And I also suggest that you already know what that thought is worth, Joanne Nicole."

. . . *Lita. Lita and its damned sixteen beads.*

. . . *"Jetah, that is not fair!"*

"Now you answer from stupidity."

Nicole bit her lower lip and slowly nodded. *Passion is a creature of rules....*

"I will go with you."

The sound of Tora Soam's footsteps receded from the room, while a new set of footsteps—familiar—entered.

"Mitzak?"

"Yes. I will be going with you to Amadeen."

"I was told. It seems, Mitzak, that Lita is playing games with us."

He laughed. "No rules?"

Nicole leaned the back of her head against the couch. "There are rules, Mitzak. There are always rules. We just don't know what they are yet. Let's just hope to hell we have sense enough to yell 'I win' before everyone else does."

That evening, at the night repast back at the Tora estate, the actor, Fanda, performed a short piece from a modern play. Tora Kia sat silently, while the "brass" giggled and applauded Fanda's performance. "The brass" belonged to the same performance company from which Fanda had come.

Nicole ate very little, and paid little attention to the merriment and conversation.

A desert of questions; only a few grains of answers.

There was a pause, and Nicole called Fanda to her side. "How may I serve you, Joanne Nicole?"

"Benbo. You must have met him, studied him."

"I did, yes."

"How is he?"

"When I left him, he was Ditaar vemadah. Since the USE captured Ditaar, I do not know."

She nodded. "Thank you."

Fanda returned to its companions and paired up with one of the "brass" named Tioct to perform a Drac love play. Nicole left the room and began feeling her way back to her apartment. In the silence of the corridor, there were footsteps following her. Nicole stopped walking; and the footsteps behind her stopped. She recognized them. "What do you want, Tora Kia? If you are Tora Kia?"

The footsteps moved to her side and stopped. "I am Tora Kia. You must believe that I was not a willing part of this game."

"I see that. What do you want?"

"Joanne Nicole, I am...confused."

"According to *The Talman*, that is the Drac's natural state of affairs."

"I suppose that is one interpretation." Tora Kia's breathing seemed uncomfortable. "There is something that...something that you should know."

"What is that?"

"That night, when I played the tidna and you came to the chamber. We sat together."

"And?"

"You touched my arm, placed your head on my shoulder—listened to my talk. I held you. It was dark."

"What are you trying to say, Kia?"

Kia's boots moved uncomfortably on the stone floor. "It is not easily said. It is no longer dark."

"It is dark for me."

"My emotions were not in control. I...lost control."

"Control of what?"

More nervous movements. "Joanne Nicole, I...I have conceived."

"Conceived? You mean...*Ha!*" And then Nicole laughed so hard it hurt her ribs. It was a release of so many things.

"This humor, Joanne Nicole. I do not understand it. I have just told you that I will have a child. This is not amusing."

"Pregnant!"

"Yes!"

"I'd make...I'd make an honest Drac out of you, Kia; but...what would your parent say!?" She felt the remainder of her way into her apartment, tears of laughter running down her cheeks.

"I *am* honest!"

"Take no offense at my laughter, Kia. You would have to be a human to understand it....Congratulations. Congratulations, and all the—ah, hah!"

She closed the door to the corridor and collapsed upon the floor in laughter.

16

Passion is a creature of rules. This does not mean do not love, do not hate. It means that where your passion limits talma, you must step outside of the rules of your love and hate to allow talma to serve you.
—The Story of Cohneret, Koda Tarmeda, *The Talman*

Enroute to Hell. Human and Drac corpses roasting over the pit that was Amadeen. Could there be a war in which no one wants peace? On Earth ancient hates still burned the Semites. The United Kingdom and Northern Ireland had long ago been absorbed by the United States of Earth. Yet the night still brought the crack of guns, screams, tears—

"Joanne Nicole, the Ovjetah would speak to you."

She softened her meditation, let the feelings of her body reach her mind and the soft hum of the Dracon Fleet Ship *Cueh* reach her ears. She pushed up from the cushion and turned toward the voice. "Aal Thaya, where is the Ovjetah?"

"Tora Soam is in the ship's screen display room with Mitzak and Tora Kia."

"I am coming."

She felt her way toward the door and pondered the absolute trust in Tora Soam, Kia, and Mitzak that she had built upon her absolute mistrust in everything. Truth is always a closely-held variable to be tested against the constants of rules. And the rules are always creatures of some group's or individual's choice; again to be tested against more rules.

Maltak Di had said it: "Truth is an elastic to be measured against elastic rules of understanding and procedure."

And faith is a form of mental blockage founded in the belief that either the truths, the measures, or both are inflexible—givens.

There was an instrument of Drac invention that could have been placed upon her back. It would have pressed dull needles against her back, letting her feel the diagrams that others could see with their eyes. She had refused it. Without her eyes, she was seeing more than she ever had seen before. Nicole could not risk something that would interfere with her vision.

She entered the screen room and sensed the others in the room with her. No one spoke. She felt her way to a couch and sat down. In a few moments a door opened and she heard Tora Soam's familiar footsteps enter the room. Tora Soam spoke, its voice evidencing passion by its cold lack of emotion. "I have this to tell you. The Dracon Chamber has cleared our mission to Amadeen. We are officially attached to the Amadeen negotiations. You will be appraised of the details in a few moments. But I want you to understand this: The principle Drac negotiator at Amadeen was named Heliot Vant—"

"No!" Tora Kia's footsteps moved across the compartment. "It is not true—"

"Heliot Vant has been murdered, and the negotiations are in shambles." There was a silence, then Kia moved back to its couch and sat down. Tora Soam spoke to them all. "Your task is to find the path we need to find peace. But if you should find it within your power to discover who murdered my dear friend, Heliot Vant, you will find my gratitude to be without limit. We shall arrive at the orbiter in less than three days. Prepare yourselves."

Mitzak spoke: "Ovjetah, your desire to find this murderer—if murder is the fact—is beside the talma to resolve this war; and might contradict it."

"Perhaps, Mitzak. None of us knows. If this murderer's reckoning serves a part of this talma, it will serve us all. If it does not, I would know the murderer's name. I am more than qualified to construct my own talma—one that will not limit the talma of peace."

Tora Soam's footsteps left the compartment. Mitzak stood and spoke. "In the space of a few seconds, the Ovjetah's view has been narrowed from the universe to a single victim. Kia, you must talk to your parent."

"I can tell my parent nothing that it does not already know, Mitzak."

"Can Tora Soam see how its view cripples talma?"

Tora Kia sat silently for a few moments. "Mitzak, your records show that you used to belong to a celibate religious sect."

"And?"

"Perhaps you do not understand the ties between those who cause and make family lines. Heliot Vant and my parent joined to conceive me."

"I did not know." Nicole could hear Mitzak take a step toward the door, and turn. "However, Tora Kia, perhaps that is why I can see how this event limits the goals and paths visible to your parent. If someone wanted to cripple your parent's usefulness by manipulating its rules of passion, that someone could do worse than to kill Heliot Vant." Mitzak turned and left the compartment.

Kia let escape a breath. "Mitzak is correct. But he does not know my parent's ability to overcome adversity." There were the sounds of Kia moving about on its couch. "Joanne Nicole, your records show that you gave birth to a child."

She could feel her face beginning to flush. "It is no concern of yours."

"How did you feel?"

"What do you mean, Kia?"

"Carrying your child, being a parent. How did you feel?"

"I spent a lot of time throwing up, a lot of time being ugly, a lot of time feeling guilty. Is that what you wanted to hear?"

"No. And I do not think you tell the whole truth. When the male, Mallik, was living; what was it like then?"

"It . . ." Joanne Nicole felt the tears come to her eyes. "It's none of your business."

"Joanne, I find it difficult to imagine how a man regards a woman; how a woman regards a man; how they both regard a child; how a human child regards its parents." Kia was silent for a moment. "I am to be a parent. Sin Vidak was composed completely from my parent's own fluids. But Heliot Vant and Tora Soam mixed fluids to conceive me. It took two beings to bring me into existence."

"And?"

"My child, in a manner of speaking, will be the same. Our fluids did not mix—"

Nicole sat upright. "Just what are you saying?"

"—but if it were not for you, I would not be carrying my child. The act of conception wreaks violence upon the parent. If I were only a few years older, the act would have killed me. My child, if it lives, will owe its life to you."

Nicole snorted out a laugh. "Kia, you owe as much to the dark and to your drugs. Perhaps more. Would you make them your child's parents, as well?"

The Drac stood and moved to Nicole's couch. Kia took her hand in its, and held it. "Joanne Nicole, what has become of your own child? The child of Mallik and Joanne Nicole?"

"I don't know." She pulled her hand free of Kia's grasp. She sat, trying to swallow her tears; then she turned her face up toward the Drac. "When Mallik was alive, it was a wonderful thing. But have you ever had a close friend die? Have you?"

"Several. Upon Amadeen."

"And what did you do, Kia?"

"Do?"

"Didn't you remove from yourself everything that reminded you of them? Even thoughts? Just to reduce the pain? Didn't you?"

Kia was silent. Then it spoke. "It is true. But a child is different than a gift, a letter, or a memory. It has a life of its own. The pain of the parent is the price to achieve the child."

Joanne Nicole pushed herself to her feet. "I don't even call it—think of it—as *my* child, Kia. That part of my life is history—dead!"

She felt her way toward the door of the compartment, but Kia's words made her pause. "You wish that it were dead, Joanne. But it is not so. Your child lives."

Nicole moved into the corridor and felt her way to her compartment.

* * *

As the ship approached Amadeen, Joanne Nicole sat and stared with her sightless eyes at the forward wardroom's unshielded viewport. She reached out her right hand and placed it upon Leonid Mitzak's arm. "Describe it to me, Mitzak."

He remained silent for a moment. "Joanne Nicole, it should not be so, but . . . I find it strange."

"What do you find strange?"

"At a certain distance Amadeen looks like Earth, Akkujah, Draco—deep blue oceans mantled with wisps and whorls of white clouds. Only now have the images of the land formations become distinct enough to tell the difference. We are facing the full light, and I can see most of the Dorado and Shorda continents. They are enormous, the Dorado filling most of the upper left quadrant and the Shorda filling most of the lower right. Between them, the Iron Channel is under clear skies."

"The strangeness?"

"It . . . it still seems familiar. Almost as though the land masses of the planets we know had been rearranged to fool us."

"Mitzak, can you make out the demilitarized zone?"

"No. But I can see large areas of both continents that look like deserts."

"Amadeen has no deserts."

"It does now."

Nicole removed her hand from Mitzak's arm and rubbed her eyes. "Have you noticed a change in Tora Soam since we learned of Heliot Vant's death?"

"Yes. As you know from your work with the computer, the autopsy showed that Heliot had ingested a large quantity of poison—pronide. It is a human way of killing. And the poison is widely distributed among USEF soldiers."

Nicole lowered her hand to her chair's armrest. "Tora Soam must realize that those facts point equally toward a human murderer or a Drac murderer's frame."

"Tora Soam, I fear, needs to see no such thing." Mitzak paused for a moment. "The joining between Heliot Vant and Tora Soam obscures many things."

"Mitzak, I know, you know, Kia knows, and more than anyone else in the universe, Tora Soam knows." Nicole sighed. "More and more I feel that Lita is out there netting us with its rules—"

"—And Tora Soam is now in Lita's net?"

"Exactly. Perhaps all of us. Which makes our positions—yours and mine—rather precarious. We are traitors to the humans, and are humans to the Dracs."

"Including Tora Soam, our only protection?"

Nicole nodded. "Yes—"

Familiar footsteps entered the compartment as the door hissed shut. It was Tora Soam. "I have been in communication with Indeva Bejuda, the acting Jetah of the Dracon Chamber's mission to the negotiations. I have been appointed the mission's representative to meet with a similar representative from the United States of Earth's mission. Joanne Nicole?"

"Yes?"

"You will assist me. We are to discuss with the humans the particulars for opening again full negotiations. Leonid Mitzak?"

"Yes, Ovjetah?"

"I want you and Kia to meet with Fourth Officer Hajjis Da. Hajjis is the officer in charge of the Drac security unit on the orbiter. Hajjis has the information regarding Heliot's death. I have already made the arrangements. You will all be issued Blades of Aydan to badge you as members of the Dracon Diplomatic Mission. Mitzak?"

"Our task, Ovjetah?"

"Find out what Hajjis knows about Heliot Vant's murder. You must learn, as well, everything that can be known about the orbiter and every being that inhabits it. Do you understand?"

"Yes, Ov—"

Tora Soam abruptly turned and left the wardroom. There was a silence in the compartment until Nicole heard Mitzak turning the control that governed the wardroom's viewscreen. "We are almost ready to dock at the orbiter."

She heard Mitzak lean forward in his chair. "What is it, Mitzak?"

"I am not certain." He leaned back. "It is a feeling."

"Describe it."

"I can see the orbiter looming out there—looking like some huge, abandoned, malevolent thing. Something asleep, but with jaws. I think I am frightened."

"Of what?"

"That the stakes in this game are higher than we imagine, and that Lita has already said, 'I win.'"

17

"I have stood where the Kathni have stood, and the universe is a different thing through their eyes. Long ago Lurrvanna taught us that logic is a creature of context and invention. If this was true for beings inhabiting the same planet for uncounted thousands of years, can it be less true for beings evolving from separate environments, inhabiting different planets?"
—The Story of Ditaar, Koda Sinushada, *The Talman*

Scant hours later, Nicole sat before a table, nervously fingering the hilt of the ceremonial dagger thrust into her waist wrap, and listened as Tora Soam introduced itself and her to the two humans negotiators. When the Ovjetah had finished, one of the humans coughed. "I compliment you on your English, Ovjetah. My name is Nikos Eklissia. The man sitting next to me is my assistant, Colonel Richard Moore."

Nicole heard Tora Soam lean back in its chair. "And, Nikos Eklissia, I also compliment you upon your command of English."

Embarrassed silence followed. Eklissia coughed, then spoke: "Our purpose here, Ovjetah—"

"All of us know our collective and individual purposes,

159

Nikos Eklissia. State your government's position."

Again Eklissia coughed. Nicole heard Tora Soam lean forward. "Eklissia, are you diseased?"

"No."

"Then I would ask you to stop blowing wind and saliva about the compartment, and to proceed with stating your position."

"Look, Drac—"

Hurried whispering came from the human side of the table; then the human spoke again. "I apologize for my nervous habit. However, Tora Soam, I can see no advantage to either of us, or our governments, in exchanging insults."

"Nikos Eklissia, our races, our worlds, our universes are in the process of preparing to continue murdering each other. Your injured sensibilities compared to the billions of dead, and the future billions that will die if we do not reach an accord on the negotiations, do not interest me. State your government's position."

"Very well. My government wants the negotiations limited to discussing the signing and implementation of the treaty accords already agreed to by Ambassador Rafiki and Ovjetah Heliot."

"No."

Another cough. "No?"

"Nikos Eklissia, circumstances have changed since that document was written. Many have died, and my friend Heliot Vant has been murdered. There will be no limits upon the subject matter of the negotiations."

"That is impossible, Tora Soam."

"You do not have the power to change your position?"

"I must consult with Ambassador Rafiki, and our gov—".

Nicole heard Tora Soam stand. "Then we have nothing more to discuss. My assistant will remain to arrange a meeting for when there *is* something to discuss."

Tora Soam's footsteps marched away from the table and out of the compartment. There was a long pause, then one of the humans stood. "I'll be damned if . . . talk to her, Colonel, and make the arrangements."

Nicole heard Nikos Eklissia's footsteps march from the compartment; and after a long moment, Colonel Moore's chuckle came from the other side of the table. "Your boss likes to hang tough, Nicole."

Nicole nodded and released her Blade of Aydan as she clasped her hands together. "And your boss is a wimp."

"I see we're going to get along just fine. Out of curiosity, why are you working for the Dracs?"

"I'm not. I'm working for peace. What are you working for, Moore?"

There were the sounds of fingers drumming upon the table. The sounds stopped. "You're blind."

"Sightless, but not blind."

"Hmmm..Well, I hope you can see this. The two negotiation teams have been hammering out the terms of this treaty for a long time. It would be signed and in effect right now, except for the Dracs breaking off everything because Heliot died. We don't want to start over from the beginning."

"Colonel Moore, I can't possibly explain to you the meaning of Heliot Vant's death. However, it couldn't have come at a worse time. I can assure you that the Dracon Chamber is both willing and able to resume the war. In addition, the Chamber and the Drac negotiating team will follow Tora Soam's recommendations."

"When should they meet again?"

"As soon as your team has the power to make decisions and agrees to take the limits off of the negotiations."

The sounds of fingered drumming again started, then stopped. "What's it going for nowadays, Nicole?"

"What's what going for?"

"Treason."

She had been waiting for the question; the same question that she had asked Mitzak a thousand years ago. Countless responses competed for the use of her tongue; but in the end she could do no more than Mitzak had done. She laughed.

Later, seated in Tora Soam's quarters next to Kia, Joanne Nicole listened as Mitzak put his conclusions before the Ovjetah. "According to the commander of the Tsien Denvedah security complement, Fourth Officer Hajjis Da, the night before the signing ceremony Heliot Vant and Ana Rafiki met informally in Heliot's quarters. Rafiki had brought with her a bottle of bourbon—"

"Explain."

"It is a beverage containing a form of the drug alcohol. Tests showed that Heliot's portion of the beverage contained the poison. There were no traces of the poison either in the bottle or in Ambassador Rafiki's portion of the beverage."

"Emmmm. A question, Nicole?"

"Yes. Mitzak, who poured the drinks, and where?"

"According to Hajjis Da's interview with Na Chanji, Heliot's duty guard, Rafiki's duty guard poured the drinks in the galley immediately off of Heliot's quarters. Na Chanji observed the human guard do this. Then Na Chanji carried the drinks into Heliot's quarters."

Nicole frowned. "The glasses—containers—who provided them?"

"The containers came from Heliot Vant's galley."

Nicole nodded. "Go ahead."

"Hajjis Da concludes that there were only four who could have administered the poison to Heliot Vant. The first is Ambassador Rafiki."

Tora Soam grunted. "The news has just been announced that Rafiki is being recalled by her government. The next, Mitzak."

"Next there is Heliot Vant's duty guard, Na Chanji. Na Chanji is dead—a suicide that took place shortly after the security commander interviewed it."

Nicole faced Tora Soam's direction. "That could indicate guilt, remorse—"

"—Or sorrow. Go ahead, Mitzak."

"Next is Ambassador Rafiki's duty guard, Ivor Kroag. He was a military police private with the USE Force." Mitzak was silent for a moment. "Kroag was transferred to the USE Forces stationed on Amadeen eight days before we arrived. He was reported killed on DMZ duty three days ago."

"And the fourth?"

"The fourth, Ovjetah, is Heliot Vant, itself. A suicide."

Kia spoke: "Probability laughs at you, Mitzak."

"I agree, Tora Kia; but possibility is another matter."

No one spoke as Tora Soam stood. Its footsteps moved about the compartment for a moment, then stopped. "Mitzak, does the interview with the human duty guard agree with Na Chanji's interview?"

"I don't know. Drac security was never allowed access to Kroag. In the same manner, the commander of the USEF military police on the orbiter was not allowed access to Na Chanji."

Tora Soam's footsteps began again. "Each player hides its

pieces of the puzzle from the other. This is of interest, since each side's behavior presumes the possibility of its own guilt. Yes, Mitzak?"

"Ovjetah, this parallel security organization rulebounds the investigation."

"Yes. That is obvious. Emmmm, let us construct the beginnings of a talma that will allow the investigation some movement." The footsteps stopped. "Nicole?"

"Yes?"

"Has the next meeting been arranged?"

"Moore and I settled on three days from today, providing the conditions you demanded have been met."

"Good. There are two additional conditions. In return for like cooperation from the Drac security team, the USEF military police must make its investigative materials and results concerning the death of Heliot Vant available to Fourth Officer Hajjis Da."

"I understand. And the second condition?"

"The recall order concerning Ambassador Rafiki must be rescinded. Rafiki will continue to represent the United States of Earth at the talks. Is there anything more? Mitzak?"

"The lists of persons on the orbiter at the time of Heliot's death, until the present, in addition to their records—as much of their records as Hajjis Da could assemble."

"Have you copied the information into the mission's central computer?"

"Yes."

"And the information I requested on the orbiter?"

"Yes, Ovjetah."

"Give me the codes. I will study them at a later date. Give Nicole the codes, as well. Nicole, do you have anything to add?"

She held the tips of her fingers to her temples. "Perhaps." She faced Mitzak. "You said that the tests determined the presence of pronide in Heliot Vant's beverage."

"Yes."

"Who did the tests?"

"Londu Peg. Heliot's personal health master."

"And Londu Peg also did the autopsy that determined the cause of Heliot's death?"

"Yes. Do you see a fifth possibility in Londu Peg?"

"Mitzak, we are relying upon nothing more substantial than

Londu's word both as to the cause of death and the evidence indicating how the poison was administered."

"Why would Londu misrepresent the truth?"

"What law of the Universe, Mitzak, *prevents* Londu from misrepresenting the truth—or from murdering Heliot? And if we doubt Londu's word concerning the cause of death, the suspects are no longer limited to those we have discussed. We are even in doubt that there *was* a murder." She turned her head and faced Tora Soam. "Where is Heliot's body?"

"At the present, it is in Sindievu on Draco. It was sent home immediately after the autopsy." The Ovjetah paused. "Emmmm. . . . I see. I shall at once order another autopsy done at the Chin Kovah in Sindievu. And now both of you may go. Kia, I want you to stay. We must talk."

"About what, my parent?"

"It is a private matter."

Nicole stood up. "There is one more thing, Tora Soam."

"What is that?"

"We know that this war is rulebound. You told me that my task was to determine how it is rulebound. To continue this investigation into the death of your friend will necessarily take away from the time I can spend on the more important problem."

"Emmmm. What law of the Universe *prevents* knowledge of the circumstances concerning Heliot's death from being a possible path to achieving the larger goal?"

Nicole held out her hand. "Mitzak, please help me to my quarters. I haven't been there since we arrived, and I am tired."

She felt Tora Soam's hand on her arm. "My view is not as narrow as you suspect, Nicole. Do not close paths simply because another wants them explored. You must have better reasons."

"Just as you must have better reasons than your friend's death to commit all of our resources to exploring only one path."

"May the morning find you well, Joanne Nicole."

She nodded, the hand released her arm, and Leonid Mitzak led her from Tora Soam's quarters.

After entering her guarded quarters, she quickly felt her way around the walls—noting each light fixture, each piece of cabin furniture—then she lowered herself upon the bed platform and stretched out, her arms over her head. She took two deep breaths, relaxed her muscles, and tried to clear her mind for sleep.

But there was something: uneasiness; questions hanging without answers; an overwhelming sense of dread. Her thoughts moved at random, the attempted suppression of a particularly demanding or disturbing thought only moving her mind to more demanding, more disturbing, areas.

Jetah Lita had delighted in inventing situations in which to place its students; each situation designed to remove mental blinders from the students, inflicting upon them the kind of mistrust that would allow the corner of a truth to be seen. And the mental blinders that were removed—fairness, right, honor, morality, good, evil, love, hate, duty, justice, freedom, oppression—were all malleable creatures composed of transitory rules.

Inventions.

And the student said, "Jetah, love is not a thing of rules; it is a thing of feelings."

Lita smiled. "And you do not see, Fa Ney, that feelings are creatures of rules?"

"I do not, Jetah."

"Do you love me, Fa Ney?"

"Of course, Jetah."

"Why?"

"I just do."

"And if all that I taught you were lies, if I constantly beat you, degraded you, and humiliated you, would you still love me?"

The student thought. "No."

"Then, Fa Ney, your feelings demand certain conditions; they require that I be a certain way, and do certain things. Your love demands that I comply with certain rules—rules *you* invented."

Fa Ney began to cry. "Does this mean, Jetah, that I do not love you?"

"I comply with your rules, child. Therefore you do love me, as I love you. Did our discussion make you doubt that?"

The student nodded. "But you love me . . . because I comply with *your* rules?"

"Yes. But that does not diminish the feeling. Under-

stand the event and the facts that govern the event, Fa
Ney. Understand your feelings and the rules that govern
them. Place your trust in such an understanding, for this
allows you to trust your feelings.

"Never place your trust in a word."

Joanne Nicole sat up, crossed her legs, and rested her face
in her hands. *"Peace" is a word representing the compliance
with a malleable set of rules. And "war." When the Tsien
Denvedah and the USE Force fight, it is called "war." When
the Amadeen Front and the Mavedah fight, it is called "terrorism," "civil conflict,"—*
*—or reach back in time for other words: "police action,"
"the troubles," "uprising,"—*
*And "murder" is a word. The Drac children who died at
the kovah in V'Butaan were not "murder victims." They were
"casualties." They died by a different set of rules than did
Heliot Vant.*

Nicole sighed, swing her legs to the deck, and stood up.
She moved toward her compartment's terminal and sat down
before it. Lita had said: *"All rules aim toward goals, and all
goals are rules aimed toward further goals."*

"A circle—a chain."

Ditaar had said, *"To understand the circle, break it and
travel in both directions until you meet yourself. To understand
the chain, understand the closest link, then travel in both directions until you run out of links."*

She sat back from the terminal. What goal was served by
Heliot Vant's death? She spoke out loud: "It prevented the
signing of the Rafiki-Heliot Treaty, it renewed hostilities upon
Amadeen, and it made possible different terms under the reopened negotiations." . . . *And all goals are rules leading to
further goals.*

"What is served by changing the treaty terms?" She reached
out her hand and felt the controls of the terminal. Finding the
proper key, she pressed it and spoke: "Joanne Nicole, voice-
receive."

The terminal toned, and Nicole spoke again: "Play document, Amadeen orbiter treaty, initialed draft." She listened to
the document. While the USE Force and the Dracon Fleet stood
only an order away from mutual destruction, and while the
Amadeen Front and the Mavedah unleashed horror and suf-

fering upon each other below, Heliot Vant and Ana Rafiki had reached an agreement.

The agreement ended the major conflict, made permanent joint USE-Drac institutions for returning captured territories, colonizing new planets, exploiting the undecided areas upon Amadeen, arbitrating war crimes and reparations, and policing in force a demilitarized zone upon Amadeen that divided human and Drac according to the territories each governed prior to the war—

Nicole stopped the terminal's voice. The treaty did not satisfy the goals of either the Front or the Mavedah. She let her chin rest upon her chest. *Tora Kia had said, the only goal to be satisfied upon Amadeen is death.*

Whether the treaty were signed or not, the fighting would continue upon Amadeen. The treaty would have continued, for a time at least, the end of the major conflict between the USEF and the Dracon Fleet. Regular forces would have been withdrawn from Amadeen . . . but the fighting would have continued.

Neither the Front nor the Mavedah could be served by either Heliot's death or the failure or renegotiation of the treaty. Both organizations were beyond diplomacy.

Who then? Whose goals are served by the failure of the treaty, or by the success of a different treaty? Neither the United States of Earth nor the Dracon Chamber could derive an advantage in continuing the war. The machines and sciences of both races showed them grinding each other down until . . .

A successful treaty would serve both Rafiki's and Heliot's diplomatic goals, as well as their personal career goals. Heliot Vant did not end its own life and Rafiki did not kill the Drac . . . unless there was something else—

What of the economic interests on Amadeen? Earth IMPEX, Dracon JACHE, Timan Nisak, and the dozen or so other companies?

Nicole shook her head. No one had made a credit out of Amadeen since the beginning of the war. Not only would the economic interests on Amadeen be served by ending the war, such service required, as well, an end to the fighting upon Amadeen. No one's interests appeared to be served by Heliot Vant's death.

"Perhaps Rafiki's duty guard did it simply because he was a human and Heliot was a Drac."

Lita had said: "The first place to look for an answer is not upon the far mountain or up in the sky. First, clear the ground beneath your chin."

Ivor Kroag had been transferred to planetside duty soon after the Drac ambassador's death. . . .

But the human poured the drinks; the Drac, Chanji, supplied the glasses and carried them in. . . .

"If Kroag did it, we're talking about some improbable sleight-of-hand." And how could Kroag assure that the poisoned drink would reach its intended victim? *Perhaps it didn't matter which one died? The death of either ambassador would have interrupted the peace process.*

Chanji?

In service of what? And if the Drac duty guard had done it, celebration would have been in order—not suicide. Dracs do not meet defeat, guilt, or shame with suicide. Suicide is the Drac talma to end unendurable pain.

—if it was suicide.

Kroag and Chanji in it together? How? Why?

She shook her head and deenergized the terminal. The negotiations were irrelevant to the terrorists upon Amadeen. Everyone else had a vested interest in the success of the treaty; and therefore in keeping Heliot Vant alive.

With her hand, she felt around the terminal for her compartment's communications link.

"Damn!"

She withdrew her hand and sucked on her right forefinger, tasting blood. Carefully reaching back, her fingers felt that the plastic work surface was nicked and scratched. She found the sharp edge of the nick that had scratched her finger, felt around it, and placed her hand upon the control to the link.

She paused as an uneasy feeling swept across her mind. It was as though the last ingredient for a complicated recipe had been acquired—the final piece of an unassembled puzzle had appeared.

What recipe? What puzzle?

She pushed the feeling from her mind as she keyed the link. "Dracon Mission communications," the link answered. "How may I serve you?"

"I wish to speak with the USE Mission communications operator."

A pause. "And your name?"

"Joanne Nicole. I belong to Ovjetah Tora Soam's party."
As long as you're going to drop a name—
"USE operator," answered a human voice.
"I would like to speak with Colonel Richard Moore. Can you tell me if he is accepting calls?"
"Wait one."
The click of a connection, a hum, then a voice. "Moore."
"Colonel, this is Joanne Nicole."
There was a brief, involuntary laugh. "What can I do for you, Major?"
Major?
"I see you've been doing a little research, Colonel."
"If the war should end, Major, there'll be a wad of bad papers waiting for you. You can count on it. What can I do for you?"
"Tora Soam has instructed me to inform you that there are two additional requirements before your boss and mine can meet to discuss reopening the negotiations."
"They are?"
"First, information regarding Heliot Vant's death must be freely exchanged between Hajjis Da and the commander of USE orbiter security."
"That would be Major Haridashi. And the second requirement?"
"Ambassador Rafiki's recall order must be rescinded."
"Hmmm. I will convey your information to Mister Eklissia. Is there anything else I can do for you?"
"Colonel, would it be possible for me to talk to Major Haridashi?"
"The only authorized line open between the two missions at the present is ours. What did you want to ask him?"
"After Heliot's death, why was Kroag transferred planetside?"
A pause. "I suppose I can answer that. We were advised that keeping Kroag on the orbiter would only heighten the animosity of the Drac contingent. It was for the same reason that Ambassador Rafiki was recalled. We are trying to keep things as cool as possible up here."
Nicole sat back from the link. "Colonel, you said you were advised."
"Yes."
"By whom?" Nicole sucked the cut on her finger.

"By indirect means, the advice came from the Ninth Quadrant observation team. The advice sounded good, so we took it."

The cut! She withdrew the finger from her mouth and imagined the webs of talman paths leading to and from the cut—a net that . . . "Thank you, Colonel." Nicole keyed off the communications link, sat still for a moment, then energized her terminal, programmed it for voice response, and listened to Mitzak's orbiter information.

The orbiter was a functional ore-receiving facility operated by a Timan crew. Neither Dracs nor humans from Amadeen had ever been there. The quarters for the negotiating teams had to be specially prepared—or had been prepared when the orbiter was originally constructed.

Nicole raced through the missions of the Dracon Chamber, USE, Amadeen Front, Mavedah, and their respective security and support units, until she reached the listing for the Ninth Quadrant Federation Observation Team.

> *Boatoam Ru Seagadu of planet Moag*
> *Cherrisin He Taam, representative of planet Aluram*
> *Darlass Ita, representative of planet Aus*
> *Hissied-do'Timan, representative of planet Timan*
> *Jerriyat-a-do'Timan of planet Timan, assistant to Hissied-do*

She halted the recording. Timan. The ore receiving orbiter belonged to Timan Nisak. And the "specially prepared quarters" were old, used.

—*Mitzak in the Chirn Kovah on Draco.*
"This is strange."
"What's strange, Mitzak?"
The Ninth Quadrant study committee voted down the invitations—"
"Just as you said they would."
"—but the vote was very close. Much closer than I expected. And Hissied-do'Timan—delegate from Timan—was the only abstention." Mitzak was silent for a long time.
"What are you thinking about?"
A pause, then the sounds of Mitzak rearranging himself in his chair. "I don't understand the reason for this abstention."

"Who can figure a Timan, Mitzak? Most of them are so wrapped up in wheeling and dealing..."

...They were one of three intelligent races that had evolved upon the planet Timan. They were called Timans because the other two races—although more numerous and physically more powerful—had been eliminated....

...Completely disproportionate to their numbers, the Timans were an economic and political power in the Ninth Quadrant Assembly....

The Timans were completely non-violent; however, the Timans knew how to use rules....

Rules.

Nicole reached out her hand and felt the work surface around her terminal. It was nicked, scratched, old. Before the negotiations, neither humans nor Dracs had reason to be housed in the orbiter. Only the Timan crew had quarters there. But the compartment was constructed and appointed in the Drac manner. The compartment had been waiting for her for a long time.

She looked up at the darkness surrounding her.

Are we that predictable?

She rubbed her eyes. The compartment had been waiting for a long time, but a Drac should be staying there, not a human. She smiled. *And not a human who had been groomed to think like neither human nor Drac.* It was a fine net of cause and effect; but Tora Soam had ripped it by bringing a human instead of a Drac.

But there was another rip in the net. Somehow Heliot's death was a mistake—perhaps an accident.

What advantage does the Ninth Quadrant have in making a failure of the peace negotiations? War is similar to a contagious disease. And no one in the Ninth Quadrant wants to catch it. The entire purpose of the Ninth Quadrant, and of the United Quadrants, is peace.

"But 'peace' is a word, and never trust a word." The Ninth Quadrant would like to have peace. But more important, the Ninth Quadrant would like to have the United States of Earth and the Dracon Chamber as members....

But when it had come to a vote, the study committee had voted down the membership invitations. Hissied-do'Timan had abstained. And now Hissied-do'Timan was a member of the Ninth Quadrant observation team. And there was another Timan member: Jerriyat-a-do'Timan. Two out of five committee members. . . .

Nicole sat back as the dark outlines of an all-encircling talma formed in her mind.

The size of it; its cruel sense of purpose; the meaninglessness of so much death and destruction; the horror—

Nicole rejected the thought. It was too bizarre; the tortured, terror-driven shrieks from the mental snake pits of a paranoia ward—And from its perspective of almost ninety-five hundred years, the secret Talman Master, Ayden of the War of Ages, spoke to her mind:

> "If talma points toward an answer, the horror of which causes you to reject the answer, then blindness is both your tool and your goal. Greatness of any kind—be it theory, plan, or horror—is not comprehensible to the mind of limits. To understand all, one must be able to accept all."

Nicole touched the hilt of her Blade of Aydan and thought of the ancient Talman Master who had made war into science. She keyed the communications link and placed a call to Tora Soam. Aal Thaya, Tora Soam's servant, answered. "The Ovjetah is in meditation, Joanne Nicole."

"Well, blast it out, Thaya. I think I have some of the answers the Ovjetah has been looking for."

"Wait please."

The link hummed for a moment, then Tora Soam's voice answered. "Joanne Nicole?"

"Yes, Ovjetah. There are some arrangements you must make. First, is the *Cueh* still docked with the orbiter?"

"Yes."

"Then you must arrange for Ambassador Rafiki, Jetah Indeva, Tora Kia, Mitzak, and yourself to meet with me upon the *Cueh*."

"It would be easier to gather this assembly here in the orbiter—upon neutral ground."

"Ovjetah, there is no neutral ground."

"No neutral ground?"

"None. And, Ovjetah, you must have the central commercial and historical computers in the Talman Kovah tied into the screen room. The human equivalent to this information must also be tied in."

"I am certain Rafiki will resist. However, I will see what I can arrange. Do you know the factors governing Heliot Vant's death?"

"I have theories. Now they must be tested."

There was a pause. "I see. . . . May the many mornings find you well, Joanne Nicole."

It knows. Tora Soam knows.

"Ovjetah, that too is a theory to be tested." She keyed off the communications link, reached out, and deenergized the terminal. She sat silent for a moment, thinking. *Audio surveillance is undetectable. Therefore, anything said in the compartment, anything that went through the terminal or the communications link is known.*

But visual surveillance still requires a lens. The Drac Mission's security sweep team would have detected the equipment for visual surveillance.

Nicole stood up, moved to the nearest wall, and began feeling her way along its surface. Her hands touched the strange warmness of a lightbar, and she gasped and wrenched it from its receptacle. Gently placing the lightbar upon the floor, she moved on to the next.

After she had removed all of the compartment's lightbars, satisfying herself that the room was dark, she placed the sleeping platform between herself and the compartment's door. She bunched up the covers on the platform and felt the form of herself that she had made.

Crouching down behind the platform, she unsheathed her Blade of Aydan and tested its point and edges with her fingers.

"Be prepared to accept all. But test the truth by forcing it to lie; test the lie by forcing it to be true."

The sounds of talking came from outside the compartment, then her communications link crackled to life. "Joanne Nicole, this is Ninth Officer Eaatna, your duty guard."

Nicole reached back and keyed the link. "What is it?"

"I have been ordered to report to the commander of the watch. There are other guards in the corridor, your door is secured, and I should be back soon."

Nicole moistened her lips. "Very well."

As the guard's footsteps moved away from the door, Nicole keyed off the link, squatted down behind her bed platform, and waited.

Hearing, smell, touch, memory.

Joanne Nicole tasted the degree of her powers as the hours passed in the dark compartment. If you can hear the fold of a single layer of cloth; if you can smell the difference between an empty room and one containing another being; if you have placed in your mind the position of everything with more accuracy than one who can see those things with light, who has the superior power in a dark room?

There was a sound in the compartment, and Joanne Nicole knew the answer. Her ears flooded her mind with data as her right hand grasped the hilt of her blade. She heard a hand brush the wall and try twice to make the wall switch illuminate the compartment. Then cloth-clad footsteps walked the compartment's deck.

Cloth-clad footsteps. An atmospheric suit. There was no sound of the door opening!

There was a hiss, a sizzle, the smell of ozone filling the compartment, a wash of heat speeding over her head. The footsteps moved toward the sleeping platform as the smells of burned cloth filled the air.

"Ehhh?"

There were more sounds of hands moving through the scorched and ashed bedclothes.

Nicole moved silently to her left, around the bed platform, until she sensed the near presence of another being. She gently placed her left hand around the being's suited right leg and, with her right hand, placed the point of her blade against the leg's covering.

"Put down your weapon, or I will open you to the atmosphere."

There was a frozen moment, then Nicole felt the heat of molten steel lace through her right shoulder. As her mind dimmed from the pain, she shoved the blade with her right hand into the creature's leg.

There was a scream, a blade of energy moving through her shoulder, a whiff of ammonia, then blackness.

18

"What are the goals? What are the intended goals? Whose goals are served by the event? Whose goals are intended to be served by the event?

"The more of the truths you acquire that you need to satisfy these questions, the closer you will be toward understanding the situations that arise between creatures. And understanding the event is but a particle away from controlling its nature and effects."

—The Story of Ditaar, Koda Sinushada, *The Talman*

The upper right quadrant of her body was numb. Her mind was filled with the scarlet vision of blood as bright heat washed her face.

Tora Soam spoke over her. "Natuch, the lights."

The heat left her face "Tora Soam?"

"Yes."

"Who was it? The one who tried to kill me?"

"Emmmm." An uncomfortable silence. "We do not know. As soon as I understood what you were going to do, I had your duty guard removed and another squad of guards prepared to apprehend whoever tried to enter your quarters. They saw no one entering or leaving."

Nicole frowned. "It was wearing an atmospheric suit. I

punctured it. Whoever it was should have been dead in my quarters."

"There was no one."

Nicole let her memories pick at the problem. "Entrance was not made through the corridor. There is at least one other entrance. The body must have been removed in the same manner." She reached out a hand and grabbed at the air until she felt Tora Soam's arm. "Ovjetah, when I punctured the suit, I smelled ammonia."

"Emmmm." Tora Soam remained silent for a moment. "Nicole, only one of the members of the Ninth Quadrant observation team would use an atmosphere containing a significant amount of ammonia. Darlass Ita of the planet Aus."

Nicole shook her head. "No. That makes no sense. Timan Nisak designed and built the orbiter. It had to be a Timan."

"Joanne Nicole, everyone on the orbiter knows that you are sightless. The one who tried to kill you could have been either Timan, human, or Drac, wearing a suit, attempting to convince you that the person was from Aus. Perhaps your assailant did not intend to kill you. The purpose of the visit might have been to cast suspicion on the Timans."

"Or a Timan trying to make it look as though someone else was trying to frame the Timans." Nicole shook her head. "Tora Soam, who else is in this compartment?"

Another voice spoke. "I am Natueh Gi, Chirn Jetah of the ship *Cueh.*"

She turned toward Tora Soam. "Where are Ambassador Rafiki and Jetah Indeva?"

"At first they were both difficult about appearing here without assistants. However, both of them should be aboard by now with their guards."

Nicole nodded. "We must all meet in the screen room." She turned her head toward Natueh Gi. "Can I get up?"

"No. You should rest. Your body has suffered greatly."

She frowned at the Chirn Jetah, then felt with her left hand. Her right arm and shoulder were covered with a smooth plastic cast.

"I think I have saved the limb."

Nicole let her head fall back to the bed. "Natueh Gi, I must be moved to the screen room."

"You should rest."

The Ovjetah grunted. "Move her. She knows what must be done."

She spoke as the bed-table began moving. "Ovjetah?"

"Yes, Joanne Nicole?"

"Is the screen room tied into the Talman Kovah's computers, and the USE's commercial computers?"

"The information from the Talman Kovah is available, but Ambassador Rafiki will not allow the connection to the USE central system."

Nicole nodded once and remained impassive as the bed-table moved down the corridor.

Hurry, Natueh Gi. There is a nightmare to discuss.

Her mind swam, and an image came to her of Storm Mountain and Ted Makai, months before the attack, in the officer's club. . . .

"Talk to me about Amadeen, Ted."

"Are you one of those who are attracted by the grotesque?"

"I want to understand." Ted Makai moved in his chair, finished his drink, then ordered another. He remained silent. "Ted, Carver doesn't talk about Amadeen. Neither do Speidel or Ghadi. No one who served there does."

"Joanne, have you ever had a deathly frightening dream?"

"Yes."

"Have you ever tried to put such a dream into words to tell to another?"

"Yes, I have."

"And has anyone who heard those words ever understood the terror of your dream?"

Nightmares. . . . I would wake in the dark, the end of a scream still on my lips; shaking, the perspiration soaking my hair and bedclothes. As a child, my mother would hug me and smile as I tried to tell her about my experience; years later, Mallik would half-listen to my hysterical tumble of words, then laugh. . . .

"No. They couldn't understand . . . they were not there in the same dream."

Makai had nodded. "Now, buy me another drink. . . ."

The moving table turned a corner and Nicole sensed herself enter a larger compartment; the ship's screen room. The table stopped, and the Chirn Jetah pressed a button, raising the upper end, allowing Nicole to face the others in the room.

And now I have to tell them the nightmare that I saw.

She released Tora Soam's arm. "No one can be in here except you, Rafiki, Indeva, and myself."

Nicole heard the Chirn Jetah, Natueh Gi, leave the room. Then the Ovjetah spoke to Ambassador Rafiki and Jetah Indeva. "My distinguished guests, it is necessary that all of your guards wait outside." Tora Soam changed the direction of its voice and addressed one of the several Dracs operating the screen room's consoles. "My apologies, but you and the members of your watch must wait outside."

The Drac operator paused. "Should we shut down the facility before we leave?"

"No. We will need it. Have your watch put the things they are working on now on temporary hold."

"Yes Ovjetah."

As the operators put their stations on hold and left the compartment, the Drac and USEF guard contingents began moving out in almost identical clouds of low muttered curses. When all had gone, the compartment door hissed shut. Ambassador Rafiki walked across the deck, stopping at the foot of Nicole's bed-table.

"You must be the traitor Moore told me about."

"I am no traitor. As Tora Soam can confirm, I am vemadah. Do you understand the meaning of the term?"

Rafiki answered. "I've read *The Talman*. I'm not sure what difference it makes what label it is one uses to commit treason. Nicole, why am I here?"

"To witness a nightmare, Ambassador. This nightmare will tell you why this war happened and what binds everyone to this war. But to do this, Tora Soam must have access to USE commercial and historical information."

"Impossible."

"Ambassador Rafiki, none of the information we need is classified."

Jetah Indeva walked up and stood next to Tora Soam. "Ovjetah, is the Talman Kovah tied into this complex?"

"Yes."

"And *our* information will be put on display for this woman?"

"As much of it as is needed."

Indeva noised a grump. "I cannot allow this."

"You have no choice in the matter, Jetah Indeva. I am the Ovjetah of the Talman Kovah. Not even the Dracon Chamber may dictate to me to what use I put information."

Ambassador Rafiki spoke. "Tora Soam, you cannot force *me* to allow the tie-in."

Nicole interrupted. "No. But there is enough information from the kovah to begin, and in beginning, perhaps, Ambassador Rafiki will see enough to want to learn more." Nicole listened as the Ovjetah took its position before one of the compartment's screen consoles. She spoke. "Represent upon the screen that portion of space governed by the USE and the Dracon Chamber."

After a few moments, Tora Soam spoke. "This view is from the planet Draco."

Nicole shook her head. "Give us a three-dimensional view centered between Earth and Draco, and make the point of view far enough away from that center that all of the territory can be represented."

"And now?"

"Highlight the planets Earth and Draco."

"It is done."

Nicole pointed toward the screen with her left hand. "This is how things stood almost twenty-one hundred Earth years ago. Humans were still planet-bound, and the Sindie under Poma had just refounded their race upon the planet Draco. Now, Tora Soam, by accelerated time progression, show the colonizations by both races until the Earth year 2050." Nicole imagined the halo of dots surrounding Draco, then a similar halo surrounding Earth.

After a few moments, Ambassador Rafiki spoke. "And this is in illustration of what?"

"This shows the patterns of colonization prior to the formal establishment of the Ninth Quadrant Federation." She turned toward Tora Soam. "Now continue at a slower progression, bringing us to the present." Nicole spoke as her mind described the dots appearing on the screen. "Beginning with the year 2050, the colonization patterns changed. Observe how each pattern seems to reach toward the other." Her mind showed her the patterns aiming at each other, coming to sharp points near the planet called Amadeen.

Tora Soam spoke. "And now?"

"And now, Ovjetah, one of those planets has been colonized

by both races. Amadeen. And all seems well until, without warning, the Front and the Mavedah are formed. Before anyone knows what is happening, three hundred worlds are at war. And the war is such that neither side can win; and the problem of the war is such that neither side can quit. The only remaining path seems to be one of mutual destruction. The interplanetary fighting will end when there is nothing to fight with and no one left to do the fighting."

Ambassador Rafiki sighed impatiently. "I see no purpose in history lessons. And there is another path: the treaty worked out by Heliot Vant and myself."

"If that treaty is implemented, Ambassador, the fighting on Amadeen will continue. No police force can hold down a population determined to make war upon itself. The Dracon Chamber has a commitment to support and defend the Mavedah; The United States of Earth has a commitment to support and defend the Amadeen Front. And every soldier that fights upon Amadeen brings the infection of war away from the planet to its home."

Tora Soam's voice turned toward Ambassador Rafiki. "This is true. Until the problem of Amadeen is satisfied, both forces will remain ready, poised to strike. And more-and-more the soldiers behind those triggers will have the horrors of Amadeen in their sights. By accident or by intent, renewed interplanetary war would only be a matter of time." Tora Soam waited for the human to speak, then continued. "Nicole, we see that we are rulebound. Do you see how?"

"Find the major commercial interests involved in planetary colonizations after 2050."

There was a moment, then the Ovjetah spoke. "Nicole, there are hundreds of companies . . . labor guilds, and immigration organizations."

"The companies provide the incentives for the labor and immigration organizations, Ovjetah. Find the link between the companies."

As Tora Soam worked the console, Jetah Indeva walked to Nicole's bed-table. Indeva stopped and looked down at her. "Why don't you simply say what you have to say?"

Nicole smiled thinly, the anesthetic in her shoulder beginning to wear off. "Jetah, Shizumaat did not *tell* Namndas that Sindie was a sphere; Shizumaat *showed* Namndas."

"Dah!" Indeva thumped at its chest with the tips of its

fingers. "I am not some callow whelp sitting before my master at the kovah, Nicole. I must have answers; not stage productions!"

Tora Soam spoke from its place at the console. "If this is truth you speak, Indeva Bejuda, then you will have no objection to receiving evidence and making your conclusions after the manner of an adult." Before Indeva could answer Tora Soam's rebuke, the Ovjetah continued. "Nicole, there is no clear pattern. However, almost seventy percent of the capital investment in the colonizations is controlled by a tangle of eleven holding companies. All of these companies are charted out of different planets—none of them members of the Dracon Chamber. We don't have commercial information on them."

Nicole nodded once. "But all of those planets *are* members of the Ninth Quadrant Federation."

A pause as the Ovjetah requested and received the information. "You are correct."

Nicole turned toward Ambassador Rafiki. "Will you allow the tie-in?"

Rafiki turned her head toward the screen. "Nicole, do you have any idea of the size of the horror you are building up to?"

"Then you see it, too, Ambassador?"

Rafiki paused for a moment, then walked across the deck until she stood next to Tora Soam. "Get me the USE mission operator."

After the USE ambassador had authorized the tie-in, Tora Soam worked over the new information. Once the information had been processed, the Ovjetah walked from the console and stood next to Nicole's bed-table. "Nicole, eighty percent of the capital investment in the USE post-2050 colonizations is divided between fourteen holding companies, none of them chartered out of USE planets."

"But all of them chartered out of Ninth Quadrant planets?"

"Yes."

The direction of Tora Soam's voice changed. "There is an entity out there . . . an entity that led the Dracon Chamber into conflict with the United States of Earth?"

"Yes."

"But it would take . . . quadrillions . . . an unimaginable command of capital and resources —" Tora Soam turned until its voice was aimed at Ambassador Rafiki. "All this points toward the Ninth Quadrant Federation itself."

Jetah Indeva barked a disgusted curse. "The human mind is haunted by conspiracies, Tora Soam. This is insane! Have this Nicole's ghosts invaded your skull, as well?" Indeva's voice aimed at Nicole. "Human, what advantage is there to the members of the federation in having half the quadrant aflame with war?"

"None."

"Exactly! And how could a conspiracy between hundreds of governments—on such a scale—be kept secret for the decades your theory requires?"

"It could not."

Indeva remained silent for a moment. "Then, Nicole . . . I do not see what you see."

"In formulating the treaty terms, were there suggestions from the Ninth Quadrant observation team?"

"Yes."

Nicole nodded. "And, Jetah Indeva, the suggestions had to do with establishing the policed demilitarized zone on Amadeen?"

Indeva breathed heavily. "That *is* the core problem of the war. Before anything else, the problem of Amadeen must be put to rest."

"No, Jetah Indeva. You are wrong—twice." Nicole struggled until she sat upright upon the bed-table. "The conspiracy you say that haunts my mind, Jetah, exists. However, it is a conspiracy of fragments—a multitude of smaller plans that together mean our destruction. Earth IMPEX operates by rules. And if IMPEX received what it thought to be reliable inside information that would benefit the company, and if one or more large investors received the same information and urged IMPEX to explore the advantage, would it be difficult to cause IMPEX to explore and then exploit a particular planet?"

"You talk of only one planet."

"Yes. But continue to feed out information on other planets, and each time the information proves both reliable and profitable, the ones issuing the information gain considerable credibility—particularly if they also command large amounts of investment capital. The companies that see where Dracon JACHE and Earth IMPEX invest their resources know from experience that their own interests will be served by following suit—" Nicole shook her head. "It was so easy. It was so damned easy to lead the Dracon Chamber and the United States of Earth into war. Our rules were gathered, and then we were led by our noses into mutual destruction. And the manipulator of these things was Hissied-do'Timan, the most influential member of the Ninth Quadrant Assembly."

Rafiki sighed, and then spoke. "Too many things point to the Ninth Quadrant. Hissied-do'Timan even made himself conspicuous by his performance as a member of the federation's membership invitation committee. If this Timan is so clever, he should have been better at covering his tracks."

"Hissied-do'Timan has gone to a great deal of trouble, Ambassador Rafiki, to make certain that both he and the Ninth Quadrant Federation are identified as the culprits." Nicole turned her head. "Tora Soam, what is Hissied-do'Timan's goal? What has he been trying to accomplish?"

"The plan is simple. At our present numbers, Hissied-do'Timan would keep us out of the Ninth Quadrant Federation. With our present populations, the USE and the Dracon Chamber have the potential to cast Timan influence in the federation into a shadow. For the Timans to allow us membership, we must, first, reduce our numbers. At our present populations, we represent a considerable voting force." The Ovjetah's footsteps moved around the compartment. "And there is more. We cannot breathe a word of what we know. If we talk, this war will become known by both humans and Dracs as caused by the Ninth Quadrant. Whether we attack the federation as a result, or not, the result will be the same. Neither power will become members of the Ninth Chamber. Nicole."

"Yes, Ovjetah?"

"This is what Hissied-do'Timan wants; to keep us from membership?"

"Yes. To their minds, we threaten Timan power."

Rafiki sighed. "If this is true, I think I see what you mean by being rulebound, Tora Soam. If the truth is known, the outrage of both Dracs and humans will either cause us to attack the federation, or remain aloof from it."

Tora Soam spoke. "Either one will serve Hissied-do'Timan as well. Even if we joined forces, we could not win a war against the combined forces of the federation. And if we are not members, that is just what the Timan wants."

"But what about the war? We cannot continue with it, yet we cannot stop it, if all that has been said is true. Tora Soam?"

"You state the situation accurately, Ambassador. Do you

have a question, Jetah Indeva?"

"Yes." Indeva's voice aimed at Nicole. "If all this is true, why can we not bring Hissied-do'Timan in front of the federation's own interplanetary court? Expose him and his vile plan to the scorn of the Universe?"

Nicole smiled. "And announce this to Earth and Draco? You will find no evidence to link Hissied-do'Timan to this plan. I think that an examination of his finances will show him living off of his stipend as a member of the assembly. I doubt if any of the company investments can be traced directly to him. He planted advice and suggestions rather than money. Even when it came to a vote in his committee, Hissied-do'Timan abstained—the very essence of fairness. The Timans are experts at covering real tracks and planting false trails. And covering his trail was not difficult. You see, Hissied-do'Timan was never in this for monetary gain. He was and is in this for what he thinks is his race's survival. Hissied-do'Timan is a patriot. Ambassador Rafiki?"

"Yes, Nicole?"

"All that I am speaking to you is the truth. Take whatever steps you must to confirm it, but you must say nothing about it. If Hissied-do'Timan's plan escapes to the news media, that knowledge will do as much damage as the plan itself."

"Who do you think tried to kill you, Nicole?"

"It's not important. The universe is full of well-meaning beings who would take on a task if they thought they were serving some brand of 'justice.'"

"What about the treaty?"

Joanne Nicole settled back upon her bed-table. "Ambassador Rafiki, Jetah Indeva; as soon as you two can arrange negotiations between only the two of you—Tora Soam, Hissied-do'Timan, and myself observing—things will be made clear. There can be no guards, deputies, or assistants, and the compartment must be made secure from listening and recording devices. Before coming to the meeting, both of you must have plenipotentiary powers to act for your governments, and you must be in direct command of your respective military forces."

Tora Soam spoke. "I bring such powers with me from the Dracon Chamber. Ambassador Rafiki?"

"I will have to discuss this with my government. Nicole, why do I need such powers?"

"You will need the power and freedom to act to resolve the problem."

She held out her hand. "Tora Soam, my anesthetic is wearing off. Have quarters been arranged for me on board this ship?"

"Of course."

"Then bring me back to Natueh Gi."

She felt the bed-table begin to move, then Tora Soam's words whispered into her ear. "Hissied-do'Timan. Is he responsible for Heliot's death?"

Nicole weakly shook her head. "No. Heliot Vant's death is the thing that endangers Hissied-do'Timan's plan. Heliot's death caused the negotiations to be reopened."

The bed-table stopped moving. "Then who?"

Nicole held out her hand. "Ambassador Rafiki, can you wait for a moment?"

"Yes."

Nicole's hand touched Tora Soam's arm. "Send for your child. Between them, Ana Rafiki and Tora Kia know."

Minutes later, freshly medicated and in her bed, Nicole listened as Tora Soam, Kia, and Ambassador Rafiki arranged themselves on couches and chairs. Jetah Indeva stood beside the compartment's door. Tora Soam spoke. "Very well, Nicole. Begin."

Nicole nodded slightly. "Ambassador Rafiki?"

"Yes?"

"Explain your relationship with Heliot Vant."

"Explain?"

"What was it like? How did you feel?"

Ambassador Rafiki was silent for a long moment. "At first we could not communicate. There were too many hostilities and false issues. But as we fought over these issues, the hostility, I think, was replaced by a degree of mutual respect. I . . . I admired Heliot very much."

"And describe what happened the night Heliot died."

"I have given that information to Major Haridashi; and I have authorized the information exchange you requested through Colonel Moore."

"Please describe it. I am more interested in the feelings than in the events."

"Very well. It had been a long, hard struggle working out

the terms of the treaty. At one point in the negotiations, Heliot suggested that the two of us meet informally to allow us to discuss and settle upon several points without our respective negotiating teams screaming charges and counter-charges at each other. The meeting was very productive."

"There were more meetings, Ambassador?"

"Yes. We managed to get more done that way."

"And your affection for Heliot grew?"

"I wouldn't call it affection. . . . Admiration. Respect." A haunted tone came into the ambassador's voice. "Perhaps it was affection. I think the feeling was mutual. Just before Heliot died, it told me that it respected me. Heliot was so proud— not only of what had been accomplished, but that *we* had accomplished it. A Drac and a human. Heliot . . . was proud of *us*."

Nicole heard Tora Soam stand and walk toward the ambassador. "You cry. You cry for Heliot Vant?"

"Is that so odd?"

"Yes, that is odd."

Nicole turned her head toward Tora Kia. "Kia, explain to them what happened."

"How should *I* know?"

"You know."

There was an embarrassed silence, then Kia spoke. "Yes . . . I suppose I do. Ambassador Rafiki?"

"Yes?"

"Just before it died, Heliot Vant became very emotional."

"Perhaps. As I said, Heliot was very proud of what we had done." She uttered a sad little laugh. "Heliot . . . Heliot even blushed."

The direction of Kia's voice changed. "My parent, it is possible to feel love . . . sexual toward a human."

Jetah Indeva snorted. "Preposterous!"

"But possible just the same, Jetah."

Tora Soam spoke. "Continue, Kia."

"Heliot Vant loved her, but did not think in such terms. After all, Ambassador Rafiki is a human. There was no reason for Heliot to think that there was cause for guarding its emotions."

"Kia, do you mean that Heliot's feelings for this woman caused it to . . . conceive?"

"Yes."

"How can such a thing be possible? And at Heliot's age it . . ."

"At Heliot's age, the act of conception would result in Heliot's death. And the empathy, love, sexual feelings . . . a Drac *can* have for a human."

"How do you know?"

"It . . . has happened before."

"How do you know, my child?"

"It has happened to me."

"Kia . . ." The Ovjetah seemed stunned. "Nicole? You and Nicole?"

"It was a strange moment, my parent. It was dark . . . and I had no reason to guard my feelings. My mind was burdened by my nightmares, and this creature in the dark offered to listen—to allow me to unburden myself. Later, she . . . thought of me as her mate, seeking her own comfort."

"But you conceived?"

"Yes. The Tora line continues."

Ambassador Rafiki stood. "Nicole, you are saying that *I* killed Heliot?"

"No, Ambassador. Circumstance, misunderstanding, age . . . love killed Heliot Vant."

Tora Soam spoke. "Nicole, what of the poison?"

"Ovjetah, Heliot Vant's death was an accident. An accident that threw an enormous random factor into Hissied-do'Timan's carefully balanced equation. The poison, I think, was a desperate attempt to salvage the equation. Perhaps Londu Peg is a Timan agent. More likely, the poison was introduced later. There are enough secret corridors on the orbiter to enable the Timans to contaminate the evidence at will. The new autopsy you ordered should confirm what Kia said."

Ambassador Rafiki stood next to Nicole's bed. "The treaty Heliot and I worked out; why does it play into the hands of Hissied-do'Timan?"

"The treaty locks all sides into the problem of Amadeen. And the treaty does not resolve the problem of Amadeen. Therefore it assures the resumption of the war and that both sides will regard future treaty negotiations as closed paths— unproductive. A continued full-scale war between the USE and the Dracon Chamber is vital to Hissied-do'Timan's plan."

Ambassador Rafiki stood silently for a long moment, then she spoke to Tora Soam. "There are many things I do not understand. However, I will go now to obtain the powers Nicole thinks are necessary." The direction of the ambassador's voice changed. "Jetah Indeva, I will keep you informed."

Nicole heard the ambassador leave the compartment. Jetah Indeva grunted and followed the human.

Tora Soam spoke. "Nicole, I feel that I should say something."

"About what?"

"So many things. . . . For one, you and Kia . . ."

Kia's voice. "Yes, my parent. It is true."

"Then, my child . . . then you must be transported back to Draco. There is too much risk here, if what Nicole says is true. The line—"

"If there is risk, my parent, it is not to me but to Joanne Nicole. I think it is clear now that the Timan understands her function here. I will remain here to lessen that risk."

"Do you . . . love the human?"

Tora Kia was silent for a long time. "No. Things are different in the light. But I—we—owe her the Tora line. To you and I she should be more than just a talma to solve a problem."

Nicole listened as Tora Kia walked from the compartment. Tora Soam stood silently for a moment, then spoke. "Joanne Nicole?"

"Yes, Ovjetah?"

"This thing Kia says. How . . . how can a human and a Drac . . ."

"Love?"

"Yes. Even for a moment."

"Ovjetah, Cohneret in the Koda Tarmeda once asked which is the stronger: love of form, or love of being."

"You lecture the Ovjetah of the Talman Kovah?"

"Remember, Ovjetah, that what your mind says is true, and what your feelings confirm as truth, are different creatures."

"Emmmm."

She closed her eyes and settled into her bed. "And now I lay me down to sleep, a pit of vipers at my feet. And if I die before I wake—"

"Joanne Nicole."

"Yes, Ovjetah?"

"I do not have your insight. But I see this much. Knowledge of the Timan's plan will serve the plan. How do we buy the silence of Hissied-do'Timan?" Tora Soam paused, then continued in a grave voice. "And there is more. If the Timan has planned as thoroughly as you think, then the orbiter is a bomb. Any solution that is devised can be countered by the simple expedient of blowing the orbiter and everyone in it to pieces and blaming the event on either the Mavedah, the Front, the USE Force, the Dracon Fleet, or the Ninth Quadrant."

"That would appear to be the situation, Ovjetah. We can only hope that Hissied-do'Timan views the situation in the same manner." Nicole pulled her cover up to her neck. "And now I must sleep. May the many mornings find you well, Tora Soam."

There was an uncomfortable silence. "And you, Joanne Nicole."

She listened as the Ovjetah walked slowly from the compartment. After the door had hissed shut, Nicole whispered to the empty room:

"And God bless us every one."

19

"Aydan," spoke Niagat, "I would serve Heraak; I would see an end to war; I would be one of your warmasters."

"Would you kill to achieve this, Niagat?"

"I would kill."

"Would you kill Heraak to achieve this?"

"Kill Heraak, my master?" Niagat paused and considered the question. "If I cannot have both, I would see Heraak dead to see an end to war."

"That is not what I asked."

"And, Aydan, I would do the killing."

"And, now, would you die to achieve this?"

"I would risk death as does any warrior."

"Again, Niagat, that is not my question. If an end to war can only be purchased at the certain cost of your own life, would you die by your own hand to achieve peace?"

Niagat studied upon the thing that Aydan asked. "I am willing to take the gamble of battle. In this gamble there is the chance of seeing my goal. But my certain death, and by my own hand—there would be no chance of seeing my goal. No, I would not take my own life for this. That would be foolish. Have I passed your test?"

"You have failed, Niagat. Your goal is not peace; your goal is to live in peace. Return when your goal is peace alone and you hold a willing knife at your own throat to achieve it. That is the price of a warmaster's blade."
—Aydan and the War of Ages, Koda Itheda, *The Talman*

The next few days saw Nicole's theory concerning Heliot Vant's death confirmed. Heliot had died by conceiving. During the autopsy in Sindievu, traces of the poison were found, but it had not invaded the body tissues. The poison had been added later. Londu Peg was questioned and cleared.

Outside the orbiter a USE military police detail found a dead suited Timan, an employee of Timan Nisak. Cause of death: a rip in the right leg of the protective suit, exposing the Timan to space's vacuum. Timan Nisak did not ask for an investigation.

On Amadeen's surface, Hita Zhan declared endless horror upon the Front as it replaced the recently murdered Akaam Jaada as First Warmaster of the Mavedah. At the same time, Charlotte Raza was leading units of the Amadeen Front in a massive assault upon the eastern Shorda continent.

On the orbiter, a new conference was called.

Hissied-do'Timan studied the screen. The image showed a small compartment in the orbiter occupied only by a rectangular table and four chairs. A chair was at either end of the table, and the remaining two chairs were on the opposite side of the table from his point of view. The Timan turned from the screen. The being standing against the bulkhead wore a protective suit.

"You are a strange person, Leonid Mitzak."

"What seems strange to you, Hissied-do'Timan?"

The Timan turned back to the screen. "A human, in the employ of the Dracon Chamber, now my personal informant. How many ends are there to play against the middle?"

"Strange sentiments from a Timan. My information has been accurate, hasn't it?"

"Yes, but you have not answered my question. Why are you here—with me—Leonid Mitzak?"

"I follow my interests."

"I pay you nothing. If you believe what you have said, then you must believe that aiding me will take the race that you admire and the race that birthed you to destruction. What other interest do you follow?"

"I think it should be obvious to a Timan."

"Explain it to me."

"Hissied-do'Timan, are you familiar with the human game of chess?"

"Of course. It is quite popular among the younger children of my planet. You would use this to illustrate something?"

"Imagine a chess board set up between us. Now the human who plays is an expert on a set of rules and strategies based on that set. However, the Drac who plays the human will win, because the Drac is an expert on standing outside fixed sets of rules. The Drac's first move would be to sweep its opponents pieces off the board."

"And, Mitzak; the Timan player? What would his first move be?"

"The Timan's first move would be to switch games."

Hissied-do'Timan looked up at Mitzak. "And?"

"My interests are served by throwing in my lot with winners."

The Timan looked back at the screen and nodded thoughtfully until the screen's image showed beings entering the compartment. The screen showed Ambassador Rafiki taking her seat at the right end of the table, Jetah Indeva taking its seat at the left end of the table, and the blind human, Nicole, seating herself in one of the center chairs, facing Hissied-do'Timan's point of view. Her shoulder was encased in a white cast. In a few moments, Tora Soam entered and lowered itself into the seat to Nicole's left.

Hissied-do'Timan leaned back in his couch. "Mitzak, they have left no room at the table for the Front or the Mavedah. You said that they understood that they are bound to the problem of Amadeen."

"I also said that they understood that Amadeen is not a problem open to solution. They know they are rulebound, and how."

The screen showed Tora Soam standing. The Ovjetah bent over, touched the table's communications link, and then spoke. "Hissied-do'Timan?"

The Timan keyed his own link. "Yes."

The Ovjetah's image straightened up. "We shall begin."

"Tora Soam, why am I the only Ninth Quadrant observer at this meeting?"

"It is a special meeting; and you are the only official of the Ninth Quadrant who has an interest." Tora Soam reached out a hand and touched Nicole's shoulder. The blind woman stood as Tora Soam resumed its seat. The blind woman spoke:

"An agreement between the Dracon Chamber and the United States of Earth has been reached. We are here to sign an amended version of the Heliot Vant-Ana Rafiki Treaty."

Hissied-do'Timan nodded. "Excellent, excellent.—But what does the amendment involve?"

"All Drac and USE regular forces will be withdrawn from Amadeen. There will be no more demilitarized zone. Amadeen will be quarantined and left to settle its own problems." Nicole smiled. "We are no longer locked into the fight on Amadeen."

The Timan examined the face of the USE ambassador. "Ambassador Rafiki, the United States of Earth has sworn to defend the humans upon Amadeen. There are promises."

Rafiki nodded, then looked into the camera. "The promises have been broken."

"Broken?" The Timan looked at another face. "Jetah Indevah!" The Timan sat forward. "What of the pledges made by the Dracon Fleet to the Mavedah?"

The Drac shook its head as it continued to look at the tabletop. "The pledges have been withdrawn. Amadeen is on its own."

"I find this . . . hard to understand—" Hissied-do'Timan studied the blind woman for a moment. "Nicole, everything appears to be decided already. What is this meeting's purpose?"

"To inform you, Hissied-do'Timan."

"Jetah Indeva, Ambassador Rafiki . . . you both must be aware that this treaty—abandoning your peoples upon Amadeen— will outrage both of your races."

Ambassador Rafiki answered, "Both Jetah Indeva and I have been granted plenipotentiary powers regarding Amadeen. Most of our peoples will go along with the treaty, because most people will go along with anything. Our governments will go along with it for two reasons: they are bound to our decision by law; and violating the treaty resumes the war. The treaty won't be popular, but it is preferable to the alternative."

"You must both know that you can never defend your actions."

Indeva faced the camera. "We know that not keeping silent would serve your plan, Timan, but talma must be observed. It will ruin me, but it will end the war. A small price."

"Your respective governments cannot afford to allow this treaty to go into effect. Both the Dracon Chamber and the United States of Earth subsist upon popular favor. Ambassador Rafiki?"

"Your words are true. Our decision may even cause our governments to be brought down. But that too is a small price. You see, both of our governments find it easier to break agreements with friends than with enemies. The price of breaking this treaty is too horrible for either government to contemplate—whatever the domestic political costs."

Joanne Nicole spoke. "Hissied-do'Timan, no matter how unpopular this treaty will be, it is still a treaty—a formal agreement between governments. Both governments will observe its terms, because failure to do so would violate laws, honor, pride, integrity, trust—" Nicole laughed. "You see, Timan, we are rulebound into this treaty. And you understand that, don't you?"

The Timan glanced at Mitzak, then looked back at the screen. "Nicole, do you not comprehend that my plan is served just as well if it becomes known?" He again turned toward Mitzak. "And the plan is also served if all of us die within the next moment. I can cause this to happen before your Mitzak can take a step across the deck." Hissied-do'Timan faced the screen. "Do you think that I am afraid to die for my race?"

"We count on it." Nicole shook her head. "You are a patriot, Hissied-do'Timan. I believe you would happily die that your race might survive."

"Then . . . what is all this? You have been outplayed at each turn. Your treaty changes nothing."

"At this moment, Hissied-do'Timan, units of the Dracon Fleet and the USE Force are moving toward Timan under orders to turn your planet into a cinder and your race into a memory. This force is under the direct joint command of Jetah Indeva and Ambassador Rafiki, and it will carry out its orders unless new orders are received. If you kill us all, those new orders cannot be sent. And we would buy your silence at the same price."

Mitzak walked across the deck, stopped next to the Timan, and held out his gloved hand. In the hand was a pink and blue capsule. Hissied-do'Timan looked up at the human as he took the capsule. "Throwing in your lot with the winners, yes, Mitzak?"

"Yes. Please wait while I call in your guards."

Hissied-do'Timan studied the capsule as Mitzak left the compartment, then he looked at the screen. "Timan is a Ninth Quadrant planet. If you attack it, Nicole, your war will be with the entire quadrant instead of with each other."

"Nevertheless, Timan would be ashes."

"Nicole, what if there are others; confederates who know the plan?"

"They will remain silent, Hissied-do'Timan. If they do not, they will look like fools. There is no evidence to connect you, the Ninth Quadrant, or Timan to the plan; in fact, there is no evidence of any plan. All of the commercial records have been . . . adjusted."

"And if I communicated your plans to your respective governments; do you not think they would strip you of your powers and call back the forces you two have sent to Timan?"

Rafiki rubbed her eyes and faced the screen. "Hissied-do'Timan, the attack group will have reached and cinderized Timan long before orders countermanding the attack can reach them." The Ambassador leaned back in her chair. "As a matter of fact, *our* orders countermanding the attack won't reach the force in time, unless they are issued quickly."

Hissied-do'Timan sat back in his couch as two Timan guards entered the compartment. One of the guards spoke. "The one called Mitzak said you wanted us to witness something, Excellency."

"Yes. Stand there and be silent." Hissied-do'Timan reached out a hand. "You . . . you will be traitors to your own peoples. Traitors!" When no one in the compartment answered, he cut off the screen and communications link. Still looking at the blank screen, he spoke to the two guards. "You will report what you see to the missions of the Dracon Chamber and the United States of Earth."

"Yes, Excellency."

"And tell the human named Joanne Nicole that the game is not yet over. Do you understand?"

"Yes, Excellency."

He examined the capsule, then placed it in his mouth and crushed it between his mandibles. *There is a lot of silence to keep*, thought Hissied-do'Timan as the light faded.

Do they have the will to keep it, I wonder....

I am able to come before the Jetai Diea to tell you this story because the silence was kept until the secret could no longer cause harm. But the silence carried Aydan's price. The Timan spoke the truth when he said that the game was not over.

Upon returning to Draco, Jetah Indeva Bejuda was censured and expelled from the Dracon Chamber. Indeva returned to its estate in disgrace and died from its own hand a year later.

The Jetai of this Talman Kovah demanded Tora Soam's resignation as Ovjetah. Tora Soam, and its child, Tora Kia, returned to the Tora estate to rear Kia's child, Tora Voe. Three years later, Tora Soam was murdered by a supporter of the Amadeen Mavedah.

Tora Kia took its child to the planet Lita and assumed a new identity. Kia entered its child in the Talman Kovah on Lita and gave lessons on the tidna. Tora Kia died four years after its child graduated from the kovah. Tora Voe is now the Jetah of this Talman Kovah here in Pomavu known to you as Hadsis Jiia. With this announcement, Tora Voe resumes its rightful name.

Ana Rafiki returned to Earth and was dismissed from the United States of Earth's diplomatic service. She lived for a year on Earth, but after the second attempt on her life by supporters of the Amadeen Front, she left her home planet and dropped from sight.

199

Joanne Nicole returned to Earth, stood court-martial for aiding the enemy, was found guilty, and was dismissed from the USE Force and sentenced to fifteen years imprisonment. After three years, her sentence was commuted for compassionate reasons and she was released. She then began a search for the child she had abandoned. While this search was in progress, Joanne Nicole founded Earth's Talman Kovah.

Leonid Mitzak, replacing with faith the talma he had helped to devise, eventually went to Amadeen in an attempt at achieving peace between the Front and the Mavedah. He was executed two days later. That was almost thirty years ago, and they still fight upon Amadeen.

Twenty years after Mitzak's death, the Dracon Chamber entered the Ninth Quadrant Federation. A year later the United States of Earth came to the end of its rebellion against entry and the USE planets became members of the Ninth Quadrant.

It was then, shortly before her death, that Joanne Nicole told me the story that I have placed before you. I offer this story to the Talman Kovah as the Koda Nusinda, the eighteenth book of *The Talman*. I do so as Ovjetah of Earth's Talman Kovah, Tessia Lewis, daughter of Mallik and Joanne Nicole.

━━━━━

Truth of nature and import of meaning are not matters determinable by a consensus. If only one being understands the meaning, the meaning is understood. If only one being sees the truth, the truth is seen.
—The Story of Atavu, Koda Sishada, *The Talman*

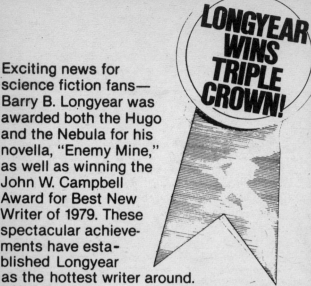